"It won't work, Felicity."

Beau stood with his feet apart, fists planted firmly on his hips. His voice was as forbidding as his stance.

Felicity tried to look innocent. "What won't work, Beau?"

"You're not going to trick me into turning my ranch into a resort for a bunch of Eastern softies."

"You stubborn cowboy!" Felicity's hand clenched. "You're impossible."

Beau's dark eyebrows quirked challengingly, but the gleam in his eyes showed he wasn't really angry this time. "*Now* you understand, Easterner."

Felicity found his complacency galling. One thing was certain: Beau DuBois was altogether too sure of himself.

Catherine Leigh says that this book is the natural outcome of living in a tiny Montana town, surrounded by beautiful mountains and friendly people. The daughter of an American Navy Admiral, she spent the first twenty-five years of her life traveling the world, but—like her heroine—she fell in love with the Western way of life. Enthusiastically encouraged by her husband and three children, Catherine is now fulfilling her lifelong dream of becoming a writer.

PLACE FOR THE HEART

Catherine Leigh

Harlequin Books

TORONTO • NEW YORK • LONDON
AMSTERDAM • PARIS • SYDNEY • HAMBURG
STOCKHOLM • ATHENS • TOKYO • MILAN

ISBN 0-373-03075-4

Harlequin Romance first edition September 1990

CHAPTER ONE

FELICITY WALDEN GRIMACED at the deep voice on the phone. "Yes, Mr. DuBois," she said, her tone soothing. "Of course, I understand. You just want us to appraise the ranch and make an offer. I realize you haven't agreed to anything yet." She rolled her eyes at Scotty, her boss, who sat perched on the edge of her chrome-and-glass desk. "Scott Realty will be glad to put together a development package for you. I'm looking forward to meeting you in a few days." Felicity dropped the receiver into its cradle and let out a groan.

Scotty gave her a grin. "This one won't be easy, kiddo," he said. "But if it's half as good as Jake says, it'll be worth it."

Felicity shook her head. "This guy sounds pretty negative about the whole deal, Scotty. He seems to think I'm going to ride into Wyoming on a bulldozer ready to level the countryside."

Scotty chuckled, almost dislodging the reading glasses precariously balanced atop his head. "Everyone thinks that about real estate developers. Especially everyone west of the Mississippi."

"Well, he certainly is that," Felicity said. "It takes three flights to get from Tampa to Jackson Hole. It sounds like the middle of nowhere."

"Close," said Scotty. "You've never been to Wyoming before, have you?"

"Are you kidding?" said Felicity. "I've never been west of Atlanta. I might as well be going to a foreign country." She reached into a drawer for her purse, then stood and pushed in her chair. "I guess at least I should be grateful they speak the same language. See you tomorrow, Scotty."

Scotty squinted at his wrist. "You're leaving early, aren't you?"

Felicity nodded, determinedly tucking a loose auburn curl back into her businesslike chignon, though she knew as soon as she stepped outside, Florida's humidity would make curls spring up all along her hairline. "I have to take Mom to her physical therapy appointment."

"How's Clarissa doing?" Scotty asked as he walked with her to the elevator.

Felicity pushed the elevator's down button. "Her therapist says she'll be able to walk with a cane soon. But speaking is still difficult for her. When she's tired, only Dad and I can understand her." Anxiety clouded her green eyes. "But I worry that Mom's pushing herself too hard."

Scotty gave her shoulder a brotherly pat. "Don't worry about your mother, kiddo. Look how far she's come since her stroke."

Felicity stepped into the elevator. "I hope you're right, Scotty." She reached to stop the automatic door from closing. "You will check on her for me, won't you, while I'm in Wyoming?"

"'Course I will," he said. "Don't I always?"

Concern lined Felicity's brow. "Wyoming's so much farther away than I usually go."

"Clarissa will be fine." Scotty pushed her hand off the elevator door. "You just keep your mind on this ranch deal."

A FEW DAYS LATER, when Felicity stepped off the plane in Jackson Hole, her breath caught in her throat. Peak after peak of the Tetons towered over the runway, their jagged rocky slopes mottled with snow and glaciers. Felicity had never seen anything so magnificent. Mesmerized, she continued to stare until the cold, biting wind made her pull her jacket around her.

Forcing her gaze away from the mountains, Felicity turned toward the terminal, surprised that such a tiny building was the airport for a world-famous ski resort. The terminal seemed so small amid miles of sagebrush and blowing brown grasses, with a few snowy hills in the distance. *The whole scene cries out for taming,* she thought, hurrying in out of the wind.

Though she hadn't expected to arrive so far from town, finding Jackson was a cinch. Felicity quickly parked her rental car, deciding she preferred walking to fighting the traffic in the town square.

She strolled through town, enjoying Jackson's cowboy facade—swinging doors, horse railings, wooden sidewalks. The place was obviously a tourist haven. No wonder Scotty was so eager to build a resort nearby. Excitement fluttered in her stomach as she thought of putting her own stamp on this beautiful but rugged land.

By the time Felicity reached Jake Conrad's realty office, a block from the center of town, she was shivering. Chimes tinkled as she pushed open the door. She looked around at the bustling activity, wondering which of the men was Jake. Then a short, balding man with a thick black mustache bounced up from the largest of the desks and came toward Felicity with a friendly smile.

"Felicity Walden?" he said, shaking her hand vigorously. "Jake Conrad. Glad you made it. Have you had a good look at our little town?"

Felicity felt instantly at home, though whether it was due to Jake's warm welcome or the warmth from his crackling wood stove, she couldn't be sure. "I didn't expect to see snow this early. It's winter here."

"Almost," said Jake. "The ski hills will open in a few weeks. But you'll still be able to see most of the ranch." He cocked his head. "Maybe not the lake though. It's pretty high."

"Not the lake?" Felicity frowned. "I can't make an offer without seeing the lake."

"Don't worry." Jake steered her through the crowded office, his cowboy boots clacking on the wooden floor. "We'll work something out. I'm sure Beau can get you up there."

Felicity sat on one of the green leather armchairs in front of Jake's desk, while he pulled out a thick folder of plats and legal documents. "It might be better if I showed you all this stuff on the DuBois ranch before Beau gets here," he said, plopping the stack of papers onto his desk.

"I studied the plats you sent me in Florida," said Felicity, trying to hide her impatience. She couldn't get a feel for this huge country from more paper. "I need to see the land before we can make a firm offer."

Jake ran a hand over his balding head. "I'd go easy with Beau when you meet him." He paused. "This ranch has been in his family a long time. Ranching's his heritage and . . . his life."

Felicity looked at him quizzically. "You make it sound like he doesn't want to sell."

Jake seemed uncomfortable. "I'd have to say that for himself, he doesn't. But Beau's younger brother, Ash, is...well, in a difficult situation. Selling the ranch seems to be the only solution. The three of them own it together, you know."

Felicity remembered the paperwork she'd gone over in Florida. "Two brothers and their mother?"

"Right. Alma." Jake nodded. "And together they've decided to sell. But it's Beau who's . . . well, I'd have to say, hesitant."

Felicity crossed her legs and began swinging one foot back and forth. Why had Mr. DuBois called her all the way out here if he was so hesitant? Oh, well, she'd handled difficult customers before. Surely it wouldn't be *that* hard to persuade him to make up his mind. She looked at her watch.

"Where is Mr. DuBois?" she asked.

"It's not like Beau to be late." Jake glanced toward the door. "I'm sure he'll be here any minute."

Four tedious hours later, Mr. DuBois still hadn't arrived or even phoned. Felicity's boredom had long since turned into irritation, then anger.

"This is ridiculous," she said at last, pushing away what must have been her tenth cup of coffee and standing up. "They won't hold my reservation at the hotel if I stay here any longer."

Jake stood, too. "I'm sure there's a reasonable explanation for all this," he said worriedly. "If Beau calls soon, maybe we can meet over dinner."

Felicity was too annoyed to sit around her hotel room waiting one minute more for this rancher to call. "I'm pretty tired, Jake," she said. "Why don't we just plan to meet tomorrow morning?"

"Fine, fine," Jake said, but his enthusiasm seemed forced. "You're staying at the Wort?"

Felicity nodded.

"If for some reason Beau can't make it, I'll call you there." He held the office door open for her. "See you at nine?"

A number of sharp retorts went through her mind, but Jake had done nothing to earn her ire. "At nine."

When Felicity arrived at his office the next morning, her irritation had been washed away by a good night's sleep. No doubt Mr. DuBois had a legitimate reason for missing the meeting yesterday. Besides, she'd planned to spend several days in Jackson anyway. One afternoon's delay could hardly be called disastrous. Feeling rested and restored, Felicity looked forward to convincing Mr. DuBois that selling his ranch was the right move for both of them.

As she stepped inside, her eyes were immediately drawn to the tall stranger lounging against Jake's desk. Dark curly hair fell across his brow from beneath a tan cowboy hat. Even without the hat, his tight faded jeans, leather vest hanging open over a chamois shirt, and cowboy boots labeled him a rancher. Felicity was used to men who wore business suits to business meetings.

The door chimes drew his attention to Felicity. His midnight-blue eyes met her green ones in an appraising stare that rocked her confidence. Felicity suddenly felt ridiculously out of place in her mohair suit and silk blouse. A half smile hovered on the cowboy's lips as he took in her Eastern clothes, his gaze lingering on her flushed cheeks before meeting her eyes once more.

Felicity felt vulnerable somehow, almost exposed. Pulling her jacket close, she tried to return his smile but couldn't seem to make her lips work properly.

"Morning, Felicity," Jake said jovially. "Come meet Beau DuBois."

As Jake spoke, the stranger uncrossed his ankles and pushed himself to his feet. He seemed to keep rising forever, growing taller as Felicity approached. When she stuck out her hand to shake his, she had to tip her head back to look him in the eye. Feeling at a definite disadvantage, Felicity wished she'd worn spike heels to minimize their difference in height. He was at least six foot four, she realized, a full fifteen inches taller than her.

Mr. DuBois removed his hat and nodded at her, ignoring her proffered hand. "Miss Walden," he said, his deep voice cool.

Felicity lowered her hand, feeling put down and defensive. "Mr. DuBois," she replied, taking a chair in front of Jake's desk. "How nice that you could make our meeting today."

Jake looked nervously from Beau to Felicity. He cleared his throat. "Let me get us some coffee," he said and scurried away.

Beau DuBois lowered himself into the chair next to hers. "I guess that's a reference to our meeting yesterday," he drawled. "I understand you were kind of ticked off when I didn't show up."

"It wouldn't hurt you to apologize for keeping us waiting," Felicity said. The words were out before she could stop them. "Or is standing women up a Western custom I haven't heard about?"

His full lips turned up in a sardonic grin, but a muscle was twitching in his cheek.

Brilliant, Felicity, she moaned to herself, she'd infuriated a potential client before she'd even begun negotiations.

"You should speak to the wife of the hunter who got lost yesterday." The half smile lingered on his lips but his tone was clipped. "She'd be surprised to find out you think our meeting was more important than her husband's life."

Heat rushed to Felicity's cheeks. "A hunter was lost?" she murmured, wishing she'd bitten her tongue.

Jake put cups of steaming coffee in front of them. "Beau knows the country around here so well," he said, "the sheriff always calls him when someone's lost. This guy's buddies hadn't seen him for twenty-four hours."

"Oh, I...um..." Felicity forced herself to meet Beau DuBois's eyes and not flinch at the irony in their dark blue depths. How had she let him get the upper hand so easily? "You found him, I hope?"

"Beau did," Jake said. "After searching about fourteen hours."

Beau nodded. "The guy has a broken leg and he's almost dead from hypothermia, but he'll make it." Disgustedly he ran a big-boned hand through his hair. "You Easterners shouldn't be allowed out here without a nursemaid."

Felicity bristled at his words but bit her lip and didn't respond.

"Do you know how many times a year this sort of thing happens?" Beau persisted.

"No, but it sounds preventable," she said, trying hard to keep her composure.

"They could prevent it," Beau said in the patient tone he might use with a child, "by staying home. Why didn't he hunt in Pennsylvania?"

Felicity turned over a palm. "I guess Pennsylvania is hunted out, Mr. DuBois. That's why a development on your ranch is such a good idea. Jackson is popular with tourists year-round."

"I'm well aware of that." Beau pulled in a long breath that tightened the red chamois shirt across his chest. "I guess we'd better get down to business, Miss Walden. Tell me why I'm better off selling my ranch to a developer instead of through Jake here."

A tickle of excitement shot along Felicity's nerves and her confidence surged back. This was her turf. "We can do much more for you, Mr. DuBois. If you're selling a ranch that's been in your family for generations, you must be interested in the bottom line."

"The bottom line?" Beau echoed. "You think money is my only consideration?"

Slightly flustered by his reaction, Felicity plunged on. "We can bring together several different buyers, each interested in developing part of the vacation market your ranch offers. Worldwide Time-Share has already expressed an interest in both the summer and—"

"Why have you involved other people?" Beau's thick brows drew together. "I thought we agreed this was a preliminary appraisal."

"It is, of course," Felicity assured him, surprised at his vehemence. "But we can't make an offer without having some idea of what various parties would be willing to pay."

"Who else did you talk to about my ranch?"

Felicity squirmed, longing to escape his cold blue stare. "We...um, I spoke to a man we've done business with before. He's interested in purchasing the dwelling. He has several dude ranches in Texas and he'd like to start one in Wyoming. He's sure Yellowstone Park will be a big draw." Felicity knew she was babbling, but something about this man unsettled her and made it hard to think.

Not a muscle twitched in Beau's rigid body. "The dwelling?"

Something in his soft voice made Felicity stop short. Jake Conrad cleared his throat, and Felicity glanced at him, glad of an excuse to look away from Beau's unrelenting gaze.

Beau's words forced her attention back to him. "You were saying, Miss Walden?"

Felicity pressed a hand to her temples. What *had* she been saying? "The dwelling...you know, your ranch house. Our purchaser says he can take any ranch house, no matter how run-down, and turn it into an elegant dude ranch in six months. So he has plenty of time to get your house in shape for next summer's tourist season."

The silence that followed seemed to stop time. Felicity looked up into Beau's frozen face, appalled to realize she had just called his home a "run-down dwelling." Every time she opened her mouth around Beau DuBois she seemed to put her foot farther in.

When she flicked her gaze to Jake he covered his eyes with his hand. Wishing the earth would open up and swallow her, Felicity looked back at Mr. DuBois. Expecting a justifiably furious scowl, she was almost relieved at the disgusted expression on his face. His tightly clenched fist was the only sign of a deeper anger.

"Mr. DuBois," Felicity said, unable to let the silence stretch on any longer. "We're only trying to put together the best package we can. If there's some part of it you object to..." Her words trailed off into the continuing silence. She took a deep breath. "Why don't we shake hands and start over?"

Jake stood. "Let me get some more coffee," he said nervously, "while you talk this out."

Beau aimed a finger at him. "Sit down, Jake." Narrowing his eyes, he turned back to Felicity. "It's too late to start over, Miss Walden. I've already made my decision."

"But how could you?" Felicity exclaimed. "You haven't even heard our offer."

"Believe me, I've heard enough. Bottom line, dude ranch, dwelling!" His voice rose with each angry word.

Unable to look away, Felicity watched Beau reach for his coffee cup and drain it. Without his icy gaze boring through her, she could look at him almost calmly. If he ever smiled and let those laugh lines crinkle up around his eyes, he'd be quite handsome, she decided. His nose was straight, his skin tanned, his teeth white and even. Corded muscles in his broad shoulders and long thighs contracted as he moved. Yes, she thought, very very handsome.

When Beau put the cup back on Jake's desk his knuckles were so white Felicity was surprised the mug hadn't cracked. "What you call the *dwelling*, Miss Walden, is my home. My great-great-great-grandfather, Jacques DuBois, put the stones in the fireplace with his own hands." He was shouting now. "Every generation of my family has added to the house."

Felicity wanted to shrink down in her chair and disappear. Other realtors in the office had stopped their work to gape at the threesome around Jake's desk.

"It's not the *dwelling*, damn it, it's the Home Place!" Beau brought his fist down on the desk with a crash. "Take your dude ranches and your A-frames and go home! It was a mistake to ask you to come." He whirled to face Jake, punctuating his words with sharp stabs at the air. "I'll sell to a rancher or I won't sell."

"But, Beau—" Jake threw out his arms. "It may take years to find a buyer for a spread as big as yours. That's why we called Scott Realty. We'll never be able to match their price."

"The bottom line, eh, Jake?" A cynical smile curled Beau's lips. "Well, the bottom line for me is the land. Cut the price if you have to. Find me a rancher or the deal's off. And don't forget—the Home Place is not for sale."

Felicity stared openmouthed as Beau turned on his heel and stormed out of the office. The slamming door seemed a signal for the other realtors to return to work, but Felicity still felt their eyes on her. Though she knew she would later feel the harsh disappointment of failure, right now all she wanted was to get out of there without further embarrassment. Standing, she reached out to shake Jake's hand.

"Thanks, Jake," she said, trying to smile brightly but feeling as if her face would crack at any moment. "Sorry it didn't work out. I hope you can find the buyer Mr. DuBois wants."

"I should have known this wouldn't work." Jake shook her hand warmly. "If it makes you feel any better, Felicity, I'm sure it wasn't anything you said. Beau scared off most of the other developers I called before they even got here. Sorry your trip was wasted."

A real smile curved her lips. "Thanks, Jake. I needed that." Glancing at her watch, Felicity was astounded to see it was only nine-thirty in the morning. It felt like midnight. "I think I'll try to catch the morning plane to Denver. Maybe I can get home tonight."

AFTER PAYING her hotel bill, Felicity turned from the registration desk and saw Beau DuBois standing in the lobby. What on earth was *he* doing here? Quickly she ducked into the shadow of the hallway, hoping he hadn't noticed her.

Peeking around the corner, she saw a middle-aged woman clinging to him. Beau looked thoroughly disconcerted as he patted the woman's back soothingly, and Felicity strained to hear what they were saying.

"Oh, Mr. DuBois," the woman said. "This morning my husband looks like his old self again, except for that cast on his leg. I can't thank you enough."

"Don't thank me," said Beau. "There were a dozen of us searching for him."

"Well, Otto and I will be eternally grateful." The woman took off her glasses and dabbed at her eyes with a handkerchief. "But . . . oh, I just can't believe it. Otto says he wants to come back here next year! Mr. DuBois, isn't that crazy?"

"No, it's not crazy." Beau's voice held such a note of gentleness Felicity almost dropped her suitcase.

Kindhearted understanding wasn't what she expected from the man who'd chewed her out in front of Jake's whole office. "After you've seen this country, it's hard to stay away. Your husband is a brave man—he needs the challenge these mountains provide." Beau's shoulders lifted in a shrug. "But next year, he ought to hire an outfitter. I could recommend a few if your husband wants."

The woman pushed her hankie into her purse. "I wish you were a guide, Mr. DuBois. Then I'd know Otto was safe."

He sounded embarrassed. "Call me Beau."

"Humph." Felicity was shocked to hear herself snorting audibly.

Beau spun around and saw her. "Ah, Miss Walden," he said, smiling sardonically. "How nice to see you again."

His appraising glance took in her flaming cheeks and open mouth, then he noticed her suitcase. In two strides, he was beside her.

"Let me carry that for you." He reached for the bag.

Felicity yanked it away. "I can manage."

"I'm sure you can," he replied. "You seem quite capable of taking care of yourself. But I don't want you to leave with the wrong impression of Western hospitality."

He leaned toward her and reached again for the suitcase. Felicity took a step back but his arm was longer. Beau wrapped one hand around the grip of her bag, and as his fingers tangled with hers, they felt warm and surprisingly gentle. The sensation flustered Felicity and made her catch her breath.

Beau lifted the suitcase from her loosened grasp. He looked at her, an amused spark in his blue eyes, that lazy half smile deepening the corners of his mouth. Felicity stared back at him, completely at a loss for words.

"Aren't you trying to make a plane?" He asked at last.

She nodded.

His grin broadened. "Then why don't you show me where you're parked?"

"Oh, um, of course."

Felicity hurried toward the exit. By now this man must think she was an idiot. She'd insulted his home, eavesdropped on his private conversation and stood gawking at him while he waited patiently to do her a favor. She could hardly wait to be on an airplane flying away from him.

When they reached her rental car Beau put the suitcase on the back seat, then opened the front door. Felicity climbed inside and fumbled in her purse for the key.

Beau leaned a forearm on top of the door, holding it open. "Sorry you had to come all this way for nothing, Miss Walden."

Was he giving her another chance? She took a deep breath. "We could start over, Mr. DuBois."

He shook his head. "I don't think so. But I would like to shake hands."

Determined to appear a good sport, Felicity took his outstretched hand, feeling rough calluses against her smooth skin. As his grip tightened into a gentle squeeze, a sensation of warmth flowed up her arm from her fingers.

"Don't blame all Wyomians for our dispute," he said, still holding her hand. "Usually we treat strangers here with the courtesy they deserve."

Felicity tugged her hand free. "I'm sure you do," she said. "But I have no doubt this will be my only visit."

He touched the brim of his cowboy hat and turned toward the curb. As Felicity started the motor and pulled into traffic, she couldn't stop glancing into the rearview mirror at the dark-haired cowboy on the sidewalk.

CHAPTER TWO

SIX MONTHS LATER, Felicity sat in her office, gazing disconsolately out at Tampa Bay, unsettled by the telephone conversation she'd just had with her father. He'd been hinting for weeks, but today he'd been downright insistent: Felicity needed to spend more time seeing her own friends. Her nightly visits with her mother, even her daily phone calls, were no longer necessary. Clarissa was fine now, and Felicity should get on with her life. Felicity knew he was right, but anxiety about her mother's health had become a habit she wasn't sure how to break.

She looked around as Scotty came through the door, carrying two mugs of black coffee. He hooked a thigh over the edge of her desk and offered her a cup.

"I saw your parents last night," he said. "Clarissa looked terrific. I'd say she's fully recovered, wouldn't you?"

Felicity gave Scotty a rueful grin. "That's what Dad just told me. Time to live my own life again, right?"

"Couldn't have said it better myself," Scotty replied. "All work and no play, remember?"

Felicity laughed. "You're a fine one to talk, Scotty. You work so hard you've been divorced three times."

"I got married three times, too, kiddo." He winked at her just as her phone began flashing, then picked up the receiver and handed it to her.

"Felicity Walden," she said into the telephone.

"Good morning, Miss Walden," returned a cultured female voice. "This is Alma DuBois. Perhaps you remember meeting my son last fall in Jackson?"

Remember? thought Felicity. *That's the understatement of the decade.* "How could I forget?"

"My son warned me you'd say something like that," Alma said. "He admits he treated you quite rudely."

"Really?" Perhaps she'd misjudged Beau. Felicity would never have expected him to admit any such thing. "Let's agree neither of us was on our best behavior."

"That sounds more than fair." Alma hesitated. "I'm not sure how much Jake Conrad told you about our family situation."

"Very little. I didn't really think I *needed* to know much to appraise your ranch." Felicity chuckled mirthlessly. "I guess I should have found out a little more before I tried to negotiate with your son."

"I doubt that would have helped. This winter, however, has made it quite clear that we must sell the ranch. Jake thinks it'll take years to find a rancher who can come close to our price. He hasn't even had a nibble yet. My son..." Alma cleared her throat. "That is, my younger son, Ash, and I wish you would consider returning to Jackson to complete the job you started last fall."

Felicity's jaw dropped. "Are you sure that's what you want, Mrs. DuBois? Has..." She wondered how to phrase this. "Has your older son agreed to the sort of development we have in mind?"

A long silence ensued. "I don't want to mislead you." There was another pause. "Our family has spent most of the winter discussing this matter. Beau is not... agreeable to your plans. However, he is willing to have you visit the ranch to appraise it and make an offer. Ash and I are hoping you can help us talk him into it. We've really decided it's the only answer. So we want to pay all your expenses. Of course, you'll stay with us here at the ranch."

"Oh, Mrs. DuBois." Felicity motioned despairingly with her free hand. "Your son and I didn't part on the best of terms. I'm the last person to talk him into anything."

"I know it's asking a lot, Miss Walden." Alma DuBois's voice was conciliatory. "But we would appreciate it very much if you'd give it a try."

Scotty was signaling wildly. "Excuse me just a moment, Mrs. DuBois," Felicity said, pushing the hold button on her phone as she glanced at him.

"If they're giving us another chance at that ranch," he said emphatically, "you get your tail out there and convince them."

"Scotty, you don't know how badly I blew this the last time." Felicity was equally emphatic. "I'd be starting off with two strikes against me."

"Don't you believe it, kiddo," he said. "You're as persuasive an agent as I've ever had. Now's your chance to prove it." Scotty rested his hands on her desk and leaned toward her. "You close this deal and I'll make you a partner."

"Your partner?" Felicity's voice rose with excitement. Then she remembered Beau DuBois's cold fury and she looked at Scotty helplessly. "Anyone else would have a better chance."

Scotty made a dismissive gesture. "If that were true, they wouldn't be calling you. Now tell Mrs. DuBois you'll be there tomorrow."

"Tomorrow?" Felicity's voice cracked. "I can't be ready to go by tomorrow."

He slid her desk calendar toward him and looked at the empty page bearing the next day's date. "Tomorrow." He pointed at her phone. "Tell Mrs. DuBois."

Felicity sighed, knowing from his tone that it would be useless to argue. Releasing the hold button, she began making arrangements with Mrs. DuBois.

THE NEXT AFTERNOON at the Jackson airport, Felicity turned from picking up her suitcase and stared into the dark blue eyes of Beau DuBois. Her heart sank. She'd hoped to have some time alone with Mrs. DuBois before she had to meet Beau again.

"Nice to see you, Miss Walden." He reached for her suitcase.

"Is this a truce, Mr. DuBois?" she asked, then wanted to kick herself. She should have been trying to ease the tensions between her and Beau, not add to them.

Beau grinned. "Let's call it a temporary cease-fire."

He headed toward the exit and Felicity had to trot to keep up with his long easy stride.

"My family decided I should pick you up so you could start wearing me down as soon as possible."

"You make it sound like a joke," she complained. "Is there any point at all to my coming here? Aren't you willing even to listen to my ideas?"

"Miss Walden, let's not kid each other." He held the door to the parking lot for her. "I couldn't live with myself if I let you tear up my land the way you want. The only reason I agreed to pay for your trip and listen to your offer is to keep peace in my family." He stopped by a large flatbed truck, opened the door and threw her suitcase behind the seat, then turned to face her. "But I didn't agree to keep an open mind."

Felicity glared at him, determined to control her temper. Did he think her time was worth so little that she could fly around the country at his behest for no reason at all? Her gaze moved to Beau's truck, and she fought a sudden urge to grab her suitcase and catch the next flight home.

The seat of the truck loomed several feet above her. Felicity grimaced, wondering how much of the mud now covering the truck would be clinging to her favorite suit once she'd climbed inside. Couldn't Beau have picked her up in some other vehicle?

"I brought the truck," Beau muttered, as though he'd read her thoughts, "because I had a load of hay to deliver." He didn't sound contrite exactly, but the edge had left his voice.

Felicity shrugged. It wasn't Beau's fault she'd chosen to wear a straight skirt. Tossing her purse onto the seat, she hiked her skirt above her knees and reached for the armrest on the inside of the door.

"Very nice," said Beau, eyeing her legs with obvious pleasure. "But not necessary."

Before Felicity could object, his large hands spanned her waist and lifted her onto the seat with surprising gentleness. The warmth of a blush crept into her cheeks as she felt the imprint of his hands lingering on her hips.

Beau climbed behind the wheel and scrutinized her, one brow raised disdainfully. "That suit probably looks great in your office," he said, shaking his head. "But I hope you brought some sensible clothes. You're going to look mighty silly wobbling around the ranch in high heels."

Felicity clenched her fists in her lap. How could he act so gentlemanly one minute and make her feel a perfect fool the next? "Of course I brought other clothes," she snapped. "Do you think all Easterners are idiots?"

An unexpected smile erased the hard look around his mouth and deepened the laugh lines radiating out from his eyes. "You said it, I didn't."

"Oh, really!" Turning her back to him, Felicity rolled down her window and took deep breaths of the sharp clean air.

As Beau drove toward Jackson Hole, Felicity watched the Tetons recede into the distance and felt her anger flowing out of her. She should never have snapped at Beau. No matter how he behaved, he was still the client. This deal meant too much to let him needle her into losing her temper again.

Glancing over at him, Felicity saw that he, too, seemed peaceful now. Beau returned her look and he nodded toward the Tetons. "It's the mountains."

"What's the mountains?"

"Don't you feel calmer now?" he asked. "Less upset by little things?"

Felicity had to bite her tongue to keep from telling him that she didn't think her future with Scott Realty was a little thing. But she *did* feel less angry. "Yes, I do."

"The land's so big and the Tetons are so overpowering, it puts everything back in perspective." He gave her a meaningful look. "That's one of the reasons I could never live anywhere else."

"You don't have to live somewhere else, Mr. DuBois," she said. "If we buy your ranch, you'll have enough money to live wherever you want."

"It would kill me to stay here and watch you destroy my land," he said bitterly.

Destroy? Felicity stared out her window at the rushing Snake River, the hills of sagebrush and granite. Beau's land, even the Tetons, could use a little civilizing, she thought. But how could she convince Beau of that when his own family couldn't? At least the rest of them wanted to sell. Beau might call it *his* land, but the ranch belonged to the family.

"Our place is another twenty miles up the Hoback River," said Beau as he veered left onto a winding road that seemed to go straight up.

"That means it's thirty miles from the ski hill!" Felicity exclaimed.

"At least." Beau's tone dripped with exaggerated patience, as though he were instructing a particularly thickheaded child. "And you should see this canyon in the winter. You can't imagine how much snow we get. The road's almost always icy."

Felicity couldn't believe anyone would actually consider driving this road with snow on it. In fact, in this big truck, it made her nervous even now. The DuBois ranch had looked a lot more accessible on the maps than it did from this narrow canyon.

Beau stepped harder on the gas pedal as he grumbled about the tourists. "Skiers die in avalanches. Hunters nearly freeze to death." He took one hand off the wheel to gesture at the granite walls around them. "Every summer some fool hiker gets lost. Can't they find a better place for a vacation?"

He drove faster and faster, not even slowing down for the sharp curves just before the bridge over the Hoback River. His body rocked as he wheeled the speeding truck around the turns. Felicity grabbed futilely at the armrest as a sudden swerve threw her across the seat almost into his lap.

"Oh, *please*, slow down!" she cried.

Her body warmed and a tingly feeling ran along her spine as Felicity realized her breast was pressed against Beau's hard chest. Quickly she disentangled herself and slid back to her side of the seat, her cheeks flaming.

"Sorry if I scared you." Beau sat stiffly, his fingers tight around the steering wheel. His eyes flicked in her direction. "You weren't in any danger, you know. I've driven trucks down this road since I was twelve."

He drove at a more reasonable speed for the next several miles and turned off the main road at a town called Bondurant. Well, hardly a town, thought Felicity. There was nothing but a post office. They bounced along the gravel road toward a beautiful fan-shaped stone mountain.

"That's Mount Nemo," said Beau, "and this is... the dwelling."

Oh, no, Felicity groaned to herself, remembering her remarks last fall about run-down ranch houses. *No wonder he was so angry. It's a log mansion.*

Beau stopped the truck in front of a large sprawling log house. Masses of bright tulips and daffodils, interspersed with clumps of alyssum, filled flower beds along the front.

A long covered porch widened into a deck, complete with hot tub, at one side of the house.

Beau took her suitcase and helped her from the truck. At the top of the porch steps he turned and pointed into the distance. "All the land you can see from here to the mountains belongs to us." His chest expanded in a satisfied sigh as he gazed at his ranch. "All the cows, too."

Felicity watched Beau's dark-lashed eyes glow as he spoke of his home. This country, she realized, was more than just a place he was fond of. It was part of him.

But when she looked in the direction he was pointing, she thought he was crazy. To Felicity, all that open space felt harsh and barren. Could she find a way to tame this hostile land? It wouldn't be easy. But as she surveyed the mountains and inhaled the fresh sweet smells of alyssum and lodgepole pine, she knew that, done right, a resort here could be her crowning achievement.

She glanced again at Beau DuBois and her stomach knotted. His relaxed air was gone and a deep sadness shone from his eyes as he looked at her. Could he read her thoughts so easily?

"C'mon, Miss Walden." He reached for the front door. "You'd better meet your allies. Looks like our cease-fire is about to end."

CHAPTER THREE

FELICITY FOLLOWED Beau past the dark log entryway into a beautifully decorated living room. Her eyes were immediately drawn to a small oil painting of an Indian woman combing her brave's hair, hanging above the massive stone fireplace. As she glanced around at the other Western paintings, at the Navaho rugs and the pottery, Felicity cringed with embarrassment.

How could she have made those stupid remarks last fall? Especially the ones about her buyer needing six months to turn Beau's home into something "elegant" enough to be a dude ranch. His house was already far more elegant than anything her buyer had in mind, and Beau knew it.

Heat crept up her neck, but Felicity forced her eyes to meet Beau's. His lips curved in an ironic grin as he watched her confusion. He was enjoying her discomfort too much to ignore. She had to admit her error.

She gestured at the living room. "This house is lovely. I— It's not what I expected."

Beau raised his brows. "Oh?" he said. "You expected dirt floors, maybe? Horse stalls in the living room?"

His sarcasm irritated her. She'd apologized; why couldn't he just drop it? Something about his taunting expression, his lazy stance, made Felicity hate to back down.

"Remember, Mr. DuBois, I hadn't spoken with your charming mother last fall." Felicity gave him a sweet smile. "You were the only ōne I'd met. Naturally I expected the, uh, dwelling to be more... uncivilized."

Beau's dark eyes narrowed as he glared at her, the sardonic gleam gone now. He compressed his lips so hard a muscle twitched in his cheek. This time, Felicity knew she'd gone too far.

The next moment—though too late for Felicity's comfort—Mrs. DuBois entered the living room. Short silvery blond hair curled around her face, setting off sparkling blue eyes that were a faded copy of her son's. Praying Mrs. DuBois hadn't heard her exchange with Beau, Felicity introduced herself.

"We all appreciate your coming out here again, Felicity." Alma's voice had an amused ring. "Even Beau."

Felicity swallowed. "I don't think Mr. DuBois—"

"Oh, let's use first names," Alma interrupted. "We're not very formal here, are we, Beau?"

Felicity steeled herself as she turned toward Beau. "If you'll call me Felicity." She tried to sound friendly, but her voice came out tight.

"Of course." Beau's smile stopped at his mouth. His gaze flickered toward the couple coming in through the archway beside the fireplace. "I'll put your bag in your room, Miss...ah, Felicity."

Felicity released a long sigh when he left. All the anger she had felt toward Beau, Felicity now directed at herself. Her foolish tongue had just made the most difficult assignment she'd ever had even harder.

Alma touched her hand. "Beau's attachment to the ranch is very strong, Felicity. I hope he hasn't been too unwelcoming."

"Not at all," said Felicity.

"Hah!"

Felicity turned to look at the woman who had spoken. Tall and willowy with flowing blond hair, she possessed the kind of sophisticated good looks Felicity associated with models. The man beside her had to be Beau's brother, their resemblance was so marked. But the open expression on his face made Felicity feel far more at ease than Beau's challenging stare. Alma introduced her younger son, Ashley, and his wife, Cherry.

"I'm so glad to see you," Cherry said, shaking Felicity's hand enthusiastically. "I thought this day would *never* come."

"It's nice to have someone on my side," Felicity answered lightly.

"Cherry's on your side, all right."

They all looked around to see Beau standing in the doorway. The tension that came into the room with him was almost palpable, but Felicity pretended she didn't feel it. She tried to respond naturally.

"If we're going to discuss the ranch . . . Beau—" she almost tripped over his name "—don't you think you should be present?"

"I hate to break up your party," he said coldly, "but we're not going to discuss the ranch now. There's plenty of daylight left. Ash and I have work to do." His expression softened as he glanced at his mother. "Did you check on Migs this morning, Mom?"

"Yes, she's fine," Alma replied. "She won't foal for a couple of weeks yet." She smiled at Felicity. "Beau's favorite mare is pregnant."

"Thanks, Mom." Beau walked through the living room and out the archway. "C'mon, Ash, " he ordered without looking back.

Ash shrugged. "I guess we'll talk tonight, Felicity."

A worried frown creased Alma's brow as she watched her sons leave the room. She turned to Felicity. "I'm sure you'd like a chance to wash up and change."

Alma led her down a hall and opened the door to an airy bedroom. Felicity's suitcase lay on a carved Chinese chest at the foot of an antique rosewood bed. A bright red canopy of watered silk matched the bedspread and curtains at the window. Felicity gawked. Could this room really be in the same house as that Western living room only a few steps away?

Alma's laugh sounded behind her. "This house has so many rooms, all built at different times by different generations of the DuBois family," she said. "I think each one cries out for its own style, don't you?"

At Alma's infectious smile, Felicity felt her own lips curving. "Oh, absolutely," she agreed. "Who wants consistency?"

"Just try to convince Beau of that," said Alma. "I try to get my hands on his room every year. He acts like it's some sort of sanctuary."

Felicity sank dispiritedly onto the edge of the bed. "I don't think I could convince Beau of anything. If I told him the sun rises in the east, he'd probably dispute it. Every time I open my mouth, I get farther from my goal."

"Now, now," Alma said patting her hand. "Don't give up yet. Beau knows we need to sell the ranch. He'll come around."

Felicity looked at Alma despairingly. "He thinks I want to destroy his land."

"Yes, I know." Alma sighed. "I guess deep down I feel that way myself. But I know this is the right thing to do for my family. You'd have to spend the winter here to understand."

"But Beau is part of the family," said Felicity. "Why does he feel so differently?"

"I'm not really sure." Alma gazed into the distance. "Since my husband died, Beau's desire to hold the ranch together has been...almost fierce." She shook herself. "Well, I'm sure you want to change out of those traveling clothes."

Obviously Alma didn't want to share any more family secrets. Once she'd gone, Felicity tried to concentrate on unpacking, but kept visualizing Beau's angry face.

Was there any point to this? she wondered, glancing out the silk-framed window at the rugged granite peaks. The contradictions here made her mind reel: silk and mountains, Navaho and Chinese Chippendale. And Beau, so cold, with so much emotion smoldering just beneath the surface.

Pulling on jeans and a bold floral print shirt, she told herself once again that she had to treat this job, and this client, like any other. Convincing Beau wouldn't be easy, but it shouldn't be impossible, either. Tough negotiations were her forte. Of course, she couldn't expect him to agree to all her plans immediately. It would take time. And first she had to get him to listen.

As she brushed her hair back into a knot at the nape of her neck, Felicity looked ruefully at her reflection in the mirror. A little more tact on her part wouldn't hurt. Painful though it was to admit, Beau's outburst last fall was partly her fault.

Returning to the living room and finding no one there, Felicity passed through the archway into a homier area that seemed to be both dining room and den. When she entered, Alma jumped up from the Shaker love seat in front of the fireplace and offered to show her around.

"I'd rather wander about on my own," Felicity explained. "Sort of get the lay of the land."

Alma led her toward the other end of the room, past a long dining table made of one great slab of oak, then through a door that opened into a mudroom filled with parkas, chaps, hats, mittens and boots of all sizes.

"You'd better borrow one of these jackets, Felicity," Alma told her. "It's a lot chillier here than you're used to."

Felicity grabbed a heavy wool shirt from a hook and followed Alma out to the back porch, which led to the huge farmyard. The nearest barn was a couple of hundred yards away. Behind the barns were a dozen or so large red sheds.

Alma pointed toward a field on the other side of the driveway. "The bulls are over there. As long as you stay away from them, you'll be safe."

Felicity walked toward the barns, overwhelmed by the size of everything she saw. Steep foothills covered with trees rose in the distance, but down here the land had an empty look. It would be okay for the dude ranch, but where would she put the skiers? How would she ever get a feel for all this land in a few short weeks?

As she approached the first barn, she turned to look back at the ranch house, dwarfed by looming snow-covered peaks. The peaceful sight forced a sigh from her throat, and she felt a renewed determination to convince Beau and complete this project.

Her eyes still on the mountains, Felicity backed slowly toward the barn. Suddenly she bumped into a warm solid mass and felt something heavy strike her leg.

Whirling around, she found Beau scowling at the leg of her jeans. His gloved hands held a large, greasy mechanical part.

"What's that?" she asked.

"It's a hydraulic pump from a tractor," he said. "I doubt if that means anything to you, but this will. I think it just ruined your pants."

Twisting her head, Felicity saw a long grease mark down back of her leg. "Oh, no. Will it wash out?"

Beau lifted a shoulder. "Kind of."

"What's that mean?"

"The jeans'll be clean enough to wear," he said. "But you'll always see the stain. Sorry, I should have looked where I was going."

Brand-new jeans! Felicity felt like swearing but when she saw how chagrined Beau seemed, she controlled herself. It was such a relief to have *him* feeling foolish for a change.

"I wasn't looking, either, Beau." She turned up her hands, smiling resignedly. "At least it wasn't my wool suit."

Relief spread over Beau's features, and his stance relaxed. Maybe this was Felicity's opportunity to get him to open up.

She pointed at the sheds. "What are those buildings? They look like airplane hangars." He gave her an unrestrained smile that deepened the corners of his mouth. "Calving sheds. We have two thousand calves here every winter, and the cows need to come inside for the birth. It's usually way below zero during calving."

"Brrr." Felicity shivered. "Poor cows."

"Just like a woman," he said, rolling his eyes in mock disdain. "What about the men?"

"The men?" Felicity said. "That's typical. The cow does all the work."

"It sounds easy to you, does it?" Beau raised a dark brow. "Getting out of a warm bed every hour all night long, going out into subzero cold, sometimes a blizzard, checking the cows in the corrals, moving the heavies inside when they'd rather stay put, pulling stubborn calves when their mothers—"

"Okay, okay." Felicity held up her hands in defeat. "That does sound like work. Do you and Ash do it all by yourselves?"

Beau shook his head. "During calving some of the hands stay in the old bunkhouses." He gestured with the hydraulic pump at the smaller log buildings.

"Those would be perfect for the dude ranch," Felicity mused.

She slapped a palm over her mouth, but the words were already out. When would she learn to hold her tongue around Beau? All the humor faded from his face and his grim look returned.

"Get this through your head, Miss Walden," he bit out. "Whatever else you talk my family into, you can forget the dude ranch. We will never sell the Home Place."

Despite Beau's anger, Felicity felt slightly encouraged by his words. He wasn't completely immune to the needs of his family after all.

"Please call me Felicity," she urged, looking at the frown line between his lowered brows and wishing she hadn't caused it.

"It doesn't matter what I call you," he said. "I won't change my mind."

"I don't understand." Felicity waved a hand toward the calving sheds. "What about that awful night-calving you just described? Wouldn't you rather stay in bed and let someone else do it?"

"You're right about one thing," Beau said. "You don't understand." He put the pump on the ground and stripped off his greasy gloves. "Let me tell you something. The only thing I like better than calving is branding and cattle drives. Ranching is what I do, and this is where I do it." He stopped to run a hand through his dark curls. "My ancestors would turn over in their graves if we sold their home for a dude ranch. It isn't going to happen."

Felicity hadn't earned her reputation by giving up easily, but she knew finality when she heard it. "What made you consider selling in the first place?" she asked curiously.

Beau put his hands on his hips. "It wasn't my idea, you can bet on that."

"You phoned us, remember?"

A long breath left his lungs. "My sister-in-law is very unhappy here." He paused. "More than unhappy, she's . . ." Beau glanced at the house, then let his gaze drift toward the mountains. "We all thought she'd adjust. But we were wrong. The constant arguing is tearing my family apart. My mother's lost ten pounds the past year. Ash is stuck in the middle. He's—" Abruptly Beau fell silent and glared fiercely at Felicity, as if she'd forced these admissions from him.

"If you agreed to sell for your family's sake why back out now?"

"I'm not backing out," he said stubbornly. "Just holding out for the right buyer."

The right buyer, my foot, she thought. *I'm traipsing all over this wilderness for nothing.* Swallowing her angry retort, she shrugged casually. "I'd be mad that you got me here under false pretenses," she said, "if it weren't for seeing the Tetons again. Everyone should see them once, don't you think?"

Beau's frown eased. The little half smile slanted his lips again. "It won't work, Felicity."

She tried to look innocent. "What won't work?"

"You're not going to get me to admit that everyone needs a vacation on my ranch."

"Oh, really!" she said impatiently. "What about all the people who'd love it as much as you do and may never get to see it?"

Beau hooked a thumb in the pocket of his jeans. "No one could love it as much as I do."

"You stubborn cowboy." Her hands tightened into fists at her sides. "You're impossible!"

"*Now* you understand, Easterner."

The wind blew a long red curl into her eyes and she tucked it back into her chignon. "You agreed to let me appraise your ranch and make an offer."

"Go right ahead," he said. "Don't let me stop you."

"I don't want you to stop me, Beau." She cocked her head at him. "I want you to help me."

"Help you?" he exploded. "Are you crazy?"

"Why not? Afraid I'll convince you?"

"Not a chance."

Beau stood with his feet apart, his fists still planted firmly on his hips. But the gleam in his eyes showed he wasn't really angry this time. He was altogether too sure of himself, Felicity thought.

"Then you've got nothing to worry about," she said coolly. "And I need someone to show me around this huge place."

"Ash'll take you."

She shook her head. "Ash is already convinced. I want you to take me."

Beau's eyes narrowed. "This is spring, Easterner. I've got work to do."

She pointed at the dim doorway behind him. "And all your work needs to be done inside that barn?"

"Well, no." He rubbed a fist along his jaw. "I'll be...around the ranch."

"Good." Felicity smiled broadly. "I'll go with you. Whenever it's convenient."

"The devil you will!"

"See?" Felicity said. "You *are* afraid."

Beau jabbed his finger at her emphatically. "I am not afraid of some little hundred-pound real estate developer who's never been west of the Divide before." He groaned, shaking his head ruefully.

Felicity almost laughed. Beau had trapped himself with his hasty words, and he knew it. When he lowered his hand, his blue eyes held a grudging respect.

"Don't expect me to take you on some guided tour," he warned her. "I'll be working. You can ride along."

Felicity gulped. She hadn't ridden a horse for years, but she couldn't back down now. "Of course I won't interfere with your work," she promised. "But you won't mind answering a few questions, will you?"

Beau expelled an exasperated breath. "This is going to be a great few weeks," he grumbled. "Won't interfere with my work, huh! Now I've got to listen to you all day and Cherry all night."

"I'd rather have you listen only to me," Felicity said. "I'll ask Cherry to leave you alone while I'm here."

Beau laughed shortly. "Cherry's been on my back for three years. What makes you think *you* can stop her?"

"Don't you worry about Cherry." Felicity tried to suppress the mischievous smile tugging at her lips. "After all, didn't I just persuade you to do something that, ten minutes ago, you'd have sworn you'd never do?"

Beau looked hard at Felicity as a range of emotions chased one another across his handsome face. Annoyance, then resignation, and finally amusement. For the first time since Felicity had met him, all the tension left his features. A deep chuckle rumbled from his chest and turned into a surprisingly pleasant laugh.

"Well, Miss Walden." Beau looked at her as though he were seeing her with fresh eyes. "I'm not going to change my mind about my ranch or about your crazy ideas, either, but it may be more of a challenge to have you around than I'd thought." His blue eyes darkened with admiration. "Shall we shake hands now and come out fighting?"

Well, the fighting would be easy enough, Felicity thought, smiling to herself.

As Beau's warm rough hand surrounded hers, she felt such a surge of pleasure, it rocked her. Beau's touch seemed to awaken all her senses and send warmth pulsing from her fingertips to her toes. Hoping the heat she felt inside didn't show in her face, Felicity glanced shyly up at Beau, afraid he'd recognize her vulnerability.

She had to catch her breath to speak. "You're on, Mr. DuBois."

Felicity tried to withdraw her hand from Beau's, not sure she wanted to, but quite sure she should. After a second's resistance, Beau released her. The intense look in his dark eyes, the way he unconsciously rubbed his right palm along his jeaned thigh, made her wonder if he'd felt the same warmth she had.

His lips looked softer and fuller somehow, the half smile less taunting. "Well, Easterner, you kind of snuck up on me that time. You've got some brains hidden behind—'' his appreciative gaze slid over her "—your more obvious charms. Next time, I'll be ready for you.''

Felicity, who minutes before had felt so satisfied with herself, watched Beau stride away from her on his long lean legs, and wondered if she'd really won this battle after all.

CHAPTER FOUR

THE SUN DROPPED toward the mountains, leaving a sharp chill in the air. Felicity entered the dining room shivering, but her spirits lifted at the sight of Ash stoking a blazing fire. Alma and Cherry sat near the hearth, sipping from steaming mugs.

"It gets cold fast here, doesn't it, Felicity?" Ash said. "You look like you could use some mulled wine."

"I'd better change first," Felicity said, pointing at her pants. "I ran into Beau at sort of a bad time."

"Good heavens!" said Cherry. "Are they ruined?"

"I'm afraid so." Felicity shrugged. "But they're only blue jeans."

"After you change," said Alma, "give the jeans to our housekeeper. Dora can get almost anything clean."

Felicity couldn't find a light switch in the darkened hallway, but she was sure her room was the third on the right, the one with the door slightly ajar. Pushing it open, she caught the scent of Beau's musky after-shave. A wide double window framing the distant mountains let in enough light for Felicity to see the simple masculine furniture. She was in the wrong room.

Uncomfortable in what was obviously Beau's private domain, she hurried out. Her room was a few doors down on the *other* side of the hall. As she peeled off her jeans, Felicity gazed distractedly out the window. Instead of red silk drapes, her mind's eye saw again that wide bare window of

Beau's, with no curtains or shades to distract him from the magnificent view.

A view of everything he wants to preserve, Felicity thought ruefully. And after their latest encounter, Beau would be more wary of her than ever, more convinced that she wanted to raze every natural acre of his ranch. She almost laughed at the brief moment of confidence she'd felt when Beau agreed to show her around the ranch. How foolish she'd been to think this was going to be easy. Felicity shook her head. Nothing about Beau DuBois would ever be easy. Stimulating maybe, challenging, even satisfying—but easy? Never!

Yet despite a niggling fear that she had lost round one, Felicity still felt warmed by their last exchange. Something had changed between them out there by the barn, something indefinable. For the first time, Beau had seen her as a whole person—not a business rival, but a woman. Whether this would make her job tougher or easier, she had no idea. But for some reason, it made her feel pleasantly excited.

A shiver reminded Felicity that she was half-undressed. Examining her shirt in the mirror, she saw that it had escaped Beau's greasy hy...hydral...whatever he'd called it. She slipped on her only pair of wool slacks and pulled a sweater over the shirt. Her Florida wardrobe was beginning to seem pretty inadequate for Wyoming. She hoped the weather wouldn't get any colder.

Back in the dining room, Felicity gratefully took the hot fruity wine Ash offered and wrapped her cold fingers around the mug while she watched flames dance in the fireplace. "My father always mulls wine at Christmas," she said. "It's hard for me to believe it's almost May."

"Know what you mean," Cherry agreed. "That's one reason I want to get out of here. It's springtime, and I can't even make a dentist appointment and be sure I'll get there. Give me the subways any day."

The edge in Cherry's voice made Felicity tense. No wonder Beau didn't want her "on his back." If Cherry didn't stop nagging, she might ruin Felicity's chance of persuading Beau to sell.

"I, um, don't want to interfere," Felicity began. "But it might be a good idea if no one mentioned the sale to Beau for a few weeks. Sort of give me a chance to tell him my ideas."

Cherry looked at her suspiciously. "You mean me, don't you?"

"Of course not," said Felicity. "I just meant—"

"That's all right. I'd do *anything* to get out of this wilderness," Cherry stated. "Including hold my tongue. I just hope it does some good. But I doubt it will."

Felicity eyed Cherry. Would she really be able to resist needling Beau? Felicity wanted to make the point more forcefully, but not in front of Alma and Ash. Explaining that she hadn't expected such cold nights, she asked Cherry if she could borrow a warm nightgown.

"Sure thing," Cherry said. "It'll be way too long for you, but it'll keep you warm."

She stood up to get it right away, and Felicity followed her. When they walked into Cherry's room, Felicity had to gasp. Even Alma's remarks about decorating hadn't prepared her for this: the fireplace was tiled, the furniture was French provincial, the walls were covered with a blue and yellow silk that matched the bedspread, and heavy blue drapes hung at the windows.

"Wow!" Felicity dropped onto a yellow chaise by the hearth. "Am I still in Wyoming?"

"Isn't it lovely?" Cherry said, her red lips curving happily. "In here, I almost forget I live in the middle of nowhere. Beau asked Alma to do these two rooms over for our wedding present."

Felicity thought again of her brief glimpse into Beau's masculine room. No wonder he kept Alma out of his "sanctuary." Cherry's room was beautiful, but Felicity couldn't imagine Beau in such a setting. She wondered how Ash felt about it.

Idly tracing a pattern in the yellow brocade, she asked, "Why don't you like living here, Cherry?"

"Because it's such a backwater!" Cherry exploded. "In winter, I can't get out of the house for months. Black ice on the road terrifies me. I can't even get to Pinedale, much less down that canyon to Jackson. Worst of all—" Cherry's clenched hands shook "—Ash goes out in huge storms to feed a bunch of dumb cows, and I don't know if he's ever coming back. I mean, he's not married to those cows—he's married to *me*. I get frantic waiting, not knowing what's happening."

Felicity felt a surge of sympathy for Cherry. "That sounds awful."

"I fell in love with Ash on a ski vacation in Jackson." Cherry smiled at the memory. "I didn't know marrying him would be like going to prison." She grimaced. "I almost left the first winter, but I couldn't. I can't live without Ash."

Felicity sighed. Just a few hours ago, she hadn't even known this family. Now she felt the wall of business reserve she usually kept between herself and her clients crumbling.

"But what about Beau?" she asked. "What will he do if they sell?"

"Oh, Beau can do anything!" said Cherry. "If he wants to ranch, he can marry Bobby Jo and run her dad's ranch."

Felicity stiffened. Nothing in Beau's behavior had led her to believe he was engaged.

"Who's Bobby Jo?" she asked tensely.

"Bud Bonner's daughter. She's been after Beau for ages." Cherry shrugged expressively. "But from what Ash tells me, Beau's not interested."

"They're not engaged?" Felicity asked, surprised at her own immediate sense of relief.

"Oh, no," Cherry replied. "Getting them married was their fathers' idea. Bobby Jo, Beau and Ash all grew up together. Actually I think she'd have married either one of them. It's just the ranch she wants—it's one of the largest in the state, you know. Come to think of it, she probably won't want Beau if he sells."

"You're kidding!" Felicity's eyes widened. "If he sells to us, he'll be rich."

"Crazy, isn't it?" Cherry threw up her hands. "I can't wait to get out of here and Bobby Jo'd give anything to get in."

Felicity couldn't help wondering about Bobby Jo and how much his father's wishes meant to Beau. She watched absently as Cherry went to her dresser and rummaged in a drawer.

"Here's the nightie."

"Thanks, Cherry." She took the high-necked pink flannel nightgown. "This feels nice and warm." After reminding Cherry, politely but firmly, of her promise to keep silent, Felicity left the room.

When she returned to the dining room, Beau was standing by the fire, his foot up on the hearth. He caught her eye as she entered and he nodded, a sardonic smile twitching his lips.

Felicity's pulse fluttered. Beau's look seemed almost a challenge—as though he'd learned all he needed to know about her this afternoon and could easily resist her persuasions. Felicity repressed the urge to tell him she had just begun to fight. After all, she wanted to win him over, not attack him.

During dinner, Felicity listened to Ash and Beau discuss their plans for the next day, but she understood very little of what they were talking about. She hoped Beau's plans included her. She could never find her way around this place without a guide.

"Okay, Felicity," Beau finally said grudgingly. "I'll be riding fences all day tomorrow. If you come along, you'll get a good look at the north range. But don't expect any special treatment. I'll be working."

Cherry gawked at Felicity. "*Beau's* going to take you around?" she asked incredulously.

Wishing Cherry wouldn't make this any harder, Felicity nodded. She cleared her throat and looked at Beau. "Riding what, exactly?"

His lips curved again into that laughing half smile, crinkling the tiny lines around his eyes. "A pickup, Easterner." He chuckled. "I should've said horses. Maybe you'd've stayed home."

"Not a chance, Beau."

He raised a brow. "You sound a lot more sure of yourself now that you know you won't be on horseback."

Felicity glared at him, tired of being the butt of his jokes. "Nothing would keep me at the house tomorrow. I came here to do a job, and I intend to do it."

Beau's shoulders stiffened. "And I intend to do mine."

Felicity batted her long lashes at him, looking as innocent as she knew how. "I wouldn't dream of trying to stop you."

Beau nodded, but said nothing. Felicity glanced at his narrowed eyes, his determinedly clamped jaw and tried to look more confident than she felt. Tomorrow she'd spend hours alone with him in the small cab of a pickup. Her stomach fluttered at the idea. She usually negotiated deals in an office, backed up by her staff—not alone with a prickly rancher who seemed to have a knack for getting under her skin one minute and making it tingle the next.

At least she'd have a whole day to persuade him to listen to her. Not that she expected him to capitulate completely. But if she exercised a little tact, something she seemed to have trouble doing around Beau DuBois, surely she could convince him to take her ideas seriously. Couldn't she?

THE NEXT MORNING, Felicity awoke feeling deliciously refreshed. *Mountain air must really do something,* she thought, arching into a stretch under the comforter.

The family was seated at the long oak table eating breakfast when she entered the dining room. Cherry's stylish Western clothes made Felicity self-conscious about her own outfit. Her green linen shirt didn't look too out of place, but next to their cowboy boots, her running shoes stamped her a real dude.

"Join us, Felicity." Beau waved a hand toward the sideboard.

Felicity eyed the array of warmed serving dishes with horror. "Just coffee, please."

"City people." Beau shook his head. "You just don't know what breakfast is all about."

Cherry pushed away a half-filled plate. "And if I keep eating like a rancher, I'll never get back into modeling."

"Good," said Beau. "You were too darn skinny when you got here."

Ash gently squeezed the back of Cherry's neck. "Now you're perfect."

Felicity watched this interplay between the brothers and Cherry, surprised at Beau's tone. She wouldn't have called it affectionate, like Ash's, but it carried none of the sharpness she'd expected. Beau was stubborn, not insensitive. She'd have to remember that if she planned to get anywhere with him.

Sunlight shone through the window onto the mirror behind the sideboard, making the whole room sparkle with light. As Felicity sat down with a second cup of coffee. Beau turned to her.

"Ready?" he asked. "The way you sip at that coffee, it'll be Christmas before we get out of here."

Felicity took a last swallow. "I'll get my things."

She returned to the dining room a few minutes later, her arms full of maps and a briefcase, with her cameras hanging around her neck. She followed Beau out to a white pickup, eyeing its muddy sides with distaste.

At least mud will wash out, she thought, throwing her papers on the seat. Beau sat behind the wheel glaring at all her paraphernalia. Then he shifted his eyes to Felicity. She struggled into the truck, catching her camera strap on the door handle. A faint warmth rose to her cheeks as she thought of being lifted into the truck yesterday by Beau's strong hands.

"You need all that?" he asked resentfully, aiming a thumb at her papers.

"I have a job to do, Beau."

"Okay, okay." He started the truck. "Just don't ask me to stop so you can get a good shot."

Felicity tried to soften him up with a smile. "What if I see an irresistible view?"

"Don't you get it yet, Easterner?" Beau muttered. "All the views on this ranch are irresistible. That's why I'm staying." He backed the truck and drove out of the yard.

THE SUN WAS TINTING the western sky pink when they drove back into the yard twelve hours later. Yawning, Beau turned off the ignition, and stretched.

"You should be tired," said Felicity, "after the day you've put in."

Beau draped his arm across the top of the steering wheel. "I didn't work hard today. I was too busy answering all your questions. I'm just sleepy because you drank most of my coffee. Maybe Dora can find us a bigger thermos tomorrow."

"I didn't mean to interfere with your work, Beau." Felicity felt abashed. "Why didn't you keep working while we talked?"

"Even for me, it takes some effort to fix fences. I can't talk and stretch wire at the same time." Beau rubbed the back of his neck. "Thanks to you, I only finished about half of what I needed to get done today."

"It looked pretty backbreaking to me," she said, thinking of Beau's bronzed chest gleaming with sweat as he pounded in the steel fenceposts and tightened barbed wire. "It's a good thing you love all this, isn't it?"

"I see you're trying to change the subject again," he muttered, opening his door.

"What subject?"

"The fact that we agreed not to interfere with each other's work. I can't spend my time jawing with you." He took off his cowboy hat and ran a hand through his tousled hair. "If you want to ride with me, you'll have to let me alone."

"It's not my fault you talked so much," she snapped, annoyed at his rebuke. "I'd ask you a single question, and you'd go on and on about ranching and the mountains and—"

Beau jammed his hat back on his head. "If it wasn't what you wanted to know," he ground out, "why didn't you stop me so we could both get back to work?"

"I didn't want you to stop." She gave a little shrug. "It was fascinating. Your life here is so different from mine. I want to understand it."

Beau's shoulders relaxed. "Well, tomorrow, let's make it more boring, huh? I've got work to do." He started to get out of the truck.

She touched his forearm. "Can I ask you one more question?"

"Why not?" he said. "The day's already shot."

"This ranch is huge," she said. "I looked at the plats before I left Tampa, but today it seemed even bigger."

Beau nodded. "And you only saw a small part of it."

"Then why can't you just sell a piece of it and buy Ash out? Why do you have to sell the whole thing?"

Beau's brow furrowed. "Half a ranch wouldn't be a paying operation, and we don't have the cash to buy him out."

"But that doesn't make sense," she said. "You just told me how big this place is."

"The ranch needs to be big, Felicity. You can't tell from the maps, but a lot of the land is unusable. Thirty-five hundred cows need a lot of pasture and eat a lot of hay." He ran a fist along his jaw. "We own this spread free and clear. I won't borrow money to buy Ash out or take out operating loans. I know too many ranchers who've lost their land to the banks."

"I'd never suggest you mortgage your ranch, Beau," Felicity protested. "Just sell us a piece of it. Then you'll have the money to buy him out. You just said part of the land is unusable. Why not sell us that part?"

Beau laughed mirthlessly and climbed out of the truck. He came around to Felicity's side and helped her out. Taking her shoulders, he turned her toward some rocky outcroppings on the hills behind the barns.

"See that cliff?" he said. Felicity had to tip her head back to see where he was pointing. "That's what I mean by unusable. Now what do you think you could build up there that anyone could live in, Miss Real-Estate Developer?"

He'd done it again—made her feel like a foolish child. "It does look a little rough up there." She shook his warm hand off her shoulder and turned to face him. "But don't write me off yet. You don't know much about my job, either. For all you know, there might be acres and acres of land you never use that would be perfect for us. If I can find it, will you listen to a proposal for developing it?"

"Dudes for neighbors?" Beau looked at her quizzically, then shook his head. "No," he admitted. "I probably won't listen to a word of it."

Felicity glared at his broad back as he strode toward the house. Looping her camera around her neck, she scooped her things out of the pickup. *Oh, yes, you will, Beau Du-Bois,* she promised silently. *You'll listen to me yet. Just you wait and see.*

CHAPTER FIVE

SEVERAL DAYS LATER, Felicity entered the dining room to hear Beau and Ash exchanging angry words. As she sat down, they stopped abruptly and glared at each other. Beau's muttered "good morning" was the only break in the tense silence.

"I've interrupted something," Felicity said uncomfortably. "Shall I wait for you outside, Beau?"

"Of course not," he replied. "Enjoy your coffee in comfort. It's the only breakfast you get." He stabbed eggs around on his plate. "We were just...discussing work schedules. My brother's been taking it easy the past few weeks."

"*I* took it easy?" Ash snorted. "While you enjoyed yourself touring the ranch with a pretty girl?"

Beau slammed his cup down, spilling coffee. "I was fixing fences!"

"Sure," said Ash. "Real efficient, too, weren't you?"

A muscle flexed in Beau's jaw but he didn't answer.

"Well?" Ash persisted.

Beau cast a sideways glance at Felicity. "I was slowed down some," he growled. "But you—" he jabbed a finger at Ash "—should have finished those cattle guards weeks ago."

"I'll finish 'em today," Ash said agreeably. "I don't know why you're so ticked off. All I said was you'd have to check the headgates. You've never minded going to the lake before."

"Oh." Felicity's mind began to click.

For days she'd been urging Beau to take her to the lake. She'd believed him when he said work kept him at the north range, where she'd seen only rolling hills of grass and sagebrush. She'd even begun to harbor a few doubts about developing such empty land.

Felicity looked at Beau with dawning comprehension. "Now I understand!" she exclaimed.

Beau's eyes narrowed. "You understand what, Easterner?"

Felicity glared back. He'd tricked her! He'd spent hours talking about life in Wyoming, spent days doing work that should have taken hours—all to keep her away from the lake. He'd been so expansive and friendly, she'd thought she was wearing him down. Now she realized he'd been wearing *her* down.

Anger at her own gullibility made her voice tight. "You sneak!"

Beau's lips twisted sardonically. "Same to you, Miss Walden."

Felicity took several calming breaths. Why hadn't she asked Ash to take her to the lake days ago? A nagging inner voice told her she'd enjoyed being alone with Beau too much, but she ignored it.

Her fingernails dug into her palms. "Did you think I would come all this way and never look at the lake?"

Beau sat ramrod straight in his chair. "I was damn sure you'd never look at it with me."

Ash chuckled. "Now you will, Felicity. You can go with him today." He held up one hand. "You gave your word, Beau. Besides, it beats the daylights out of putting in cattle guards, and you know it."

Beau scowled at the broad smile spreading over his brother's face. "You could have made it up there days ago."

"'Course I could," said Ash.

Beau's gaze moved to Felicity, then back to Ash. Suddenly the stiffness left his shoulders and a laugh smoothed away his frown. "A table full of sneaks," he said, pushing back his chair. "Okay, Easterner, let's go."

Felicity was too annoyed with herself to give in as gracefully as Beau had. Scotty would never have been taken in so easily. *Because,* persisted that inner voice, *Scotty wouldn't be taken in by a handsome face or a muscular sweat-streaked chest.*

Vowing to let nothing distract her today, Felicity followed Beau out to the pickup. She stared straight ahead, avoiding his eyes and the smile that could melt her determination. Suddenly Beau's hand grasped her chin and turned her face to him. The amusement she read in his blue eyes made her feel like a fool—again.

"Hey, Easterner." Beau's voice was thick with laughter. "Do you think I'm stupid just because I work with my hands?"

As he released her, his hand brushed her jaw, making her skin tingle. His rough fingers felt smooth and gentle on her flesh. Was this another tactic? Felicity jerked her head away.

She glared at the knowing look in his eyes. "I think *I'm* stupid for listening to you."

"You seem to have a low opinion of ranchers." Beau shrugged. "But that's okay. I have a low opinion of real estate developers."

"Let's not talk today." Felicity turned her attention to the mountains. "You do your work, I'll do mine."

"Don't expect me to enjoy watching you work at my lake." His lazy laughing tone was gone. "I never planned to take you there."

Felicity opened her mouth to respond, then closed it. Her confidence was at a low ebb. This wouldn't be a good time to get into another debate with Beau about whether she could preserve the natural beauty of his land. Sighing deeply, Felicity realized she'd been wasting her breath arguing with Beau.

The road curved sharply and began a steep climb, rapidly leaving the sagebrush behind. Felicity felt almost claustrophobic as the tall evergreens that seemed to press in on them made the twisting road even narrower.

But when Beau finally stopped the truck by the shore of a sparkling mountain lake, she gasped with pleasure.

Before she could get out, Beau grabbed her shoulder and pointed toward the water. A deer and its fawn strutted out from the trees down to the shore. Silently Felicity and Beau watched the animals drink, then amble back into the woods.

Beau folded his arms across his chest. "Where do you think those animals will go if you have your way up here?"

"Beau, I . . ." Felicity bit her lip. She had no answer for him.

"I'm going to the dam."

Felicity leaned against the truck, staring gloomily at Beau's retreating back. But she noticed a tiny crescent beach on the lake shore and walked slowly toward it. Sitting on a sun-warmed boulder, she picked a buttercup, twisting its stem through her fingers. Ice glinted in the shallow bays, and Felicity wondered when the lake warmed up enough for swimming. A peaty smell rose from the spring-damp turf.

Darn Beau DuBois—this lake would make a perfect resort site! Felicity closed her eyes and lifted her face to the sun, mentally planning secluded deluxe cabins.

"Pretty idyllic, huh?"

Felicity's eyes flew open and she stared into Beau's wary face. His forced smile didn't hide the tightness around his lips. He wouldn't, she realized instantly, want to hear her building plans.

She made room for him on the boulder. "Do you come up here often, Beau?"

"We have to check the headgates every spring. In summer, we come to turn the water on and off for irrigating."

He stretched his long legs out in front of him, crossing them at the ankle. "In winter, the road's impassable. But I always spend a few nights here in the summer."

Felicity looked around. "In a cabin?"

Beau rolled his eyes. "In a sleeping bag, Easterner."

Felicity watched diamonds of sunlight sparkle on the water. "You don't use the lake much, Beau. If there were a few cabins around it, hidden in the trees, what difference would it make?"

The angry spark in his eyes flamed. Felicity groaned inwardly. She should never have tried to talk to him here.

"Even if I believed you would stop with a few cabins," Beau grated, "which I don't, I still wouldn't agree. I've come here every summer since I was four years old. It's not just...idyllic. We need the water. Animals need it. Your tourists don't. They can get their suntans somewhere else."

Felicity stood up and faced him, arms akimbo. "You're the most unreasonable man I've ever met. You won't even—"

Suddenly Beau jumped up and grabbed her wrist. "C'mon, Felicity."

Felicity ignored the note of command in his voice and tugged, trying uselessly to free her hand. "I'll stay here as long as I want. I'm not hurting your precious lake." Beau gave her wrist a strong jerk but Felicity dug in her heels. "Let me go!"

Cursing under his breath, Beau wrapped his arm around her hips and threw her over his shoulder. Enraged, Felicity pounded on his back, while he strode swiftly toward the truck.

"Put me down!" she cried.

In a few long steps, Beau reached the pickup, opened the door and flopped her off his shoulder onto the seat. Bouncing forward, Felicity banged her head against the wheel. Beau climbed in, slammed the door behind him and released a gusty breath.

"Look, Felicity."

Holding a hand to her throbbing head, Felicity peered across the meadow. Right behind the boulder where she'd sat stood two huge shaggy brown...things! They looked like gangly horses, only much bigger. The larger of the two glared at them, snorting and pawing the ground.

"Never trust a moose," said Beau. "Especially one with a calf."

Felicity rested her pounding head against the seat. "Thanks for the rescue. I guess." She tried to smile, but her head hurt too much.

"Sorry it was so rough." Beau looked thoroughly chagrined. "I didn't mean to hurt you. I just wanted you in the truck."

"I'm all right."

Beau reached over to carefully feel her head. When his groping fingers found the bump beneath her hair, she winced and pulled away.

"Ouch."

"That's quite a lump." Beau's brow was furrowed. "You should loosen your hair. That tight knot must be making it hurt worse."

"I'm fine."

Beau took her arms and pulled her across the seat. Leaning her against him, he bent her head with one hand and began removing pins from her chignon with the other.

Felicity slapped at his hands. "Beau, stop it."

"Hold still," he ordered.

When he'd taken out all the pins, he combed his fingers through her long hair, loosening it from her head. The gentle movement of his hands against her scalp made Felicity's muscles seem to dissolve.

Beau's voice was husky when he spoke. "Your hair is too nice to keep tied up in that schoolteacher knot anyway. Why don't you wear it like this?" He ran his fingers down its length.

Felicity could barely form the words from her suddenly dry throat. "It's not businesslike."

"No, thank goodness," Beau murmured. He turned her gently toward him. "I should check your pupils to be sure you don't have a concussion."

"Don't be silly." Felicity held him away with a hand against his chest. "I just bumped my head."

"You bumped it hard," said Beau. "It won't hurt to check."

"Oh, all right."

Beau placed his hands on either side of Felicity's face, shielding her eyes from the light. He leaned so close that all she could see was his dark eyes in front of hers. His warm breath feathered her cheeks and she inhaled his musky male scent. She could almost feel his lips touching hers. Her heart pounded against her ribs and her breathing grew shallow. Suddenly, Beau pulled back from her, though his hands still cradled her face. "Your eyes react normally to light."

Beau's words seemed meaningless. "My eyes?" she murmured.

"Your pupils." Beau's voice sounded odd. His fingers traced the outline of her jaw. "They contract in the light."

"Oh. Good." Then why did she feel so off balance? She blinked. "Isn't it time we—?"

Beau straightened abruptly. "It sure is."

Without another word, he turned the truck and started down the mountain. Felicity leaned back, letting her pulse return to normal. It was just fear of the moose that made her heart pound like this, she assured herself.

Though her head felt fine after lunch, Alma insisted Felicity spend the afternoon resting. Away from Beau's disquieting presence and stretched comfortably on her bed, Felicity mused about the lake. The thought of turning that beautiful, idyllic spot into an isolated wilderness-theme resort excited her tremendously. Couldn't Beau see this was the solution to his family's dilemma?

Scott Realty would purchase the lake, Beau and Alma could buy Ash out, and her resort would be far enough from Beau that he'd never have to see it. Well, almost never. Of course, the area wouldn't be *quite* as pristine, Felicity admitted. She pursed her lips grimly. Beau would just have to compromise, that was all. The only question left in her mind was: Would Scotty still think she'd earned her partnership?

That night after dinner, Beau led Felicity to a large room, furnished as an office so that she could use the phone. "We don't come in here much," he said, pulling out the desk chair for her. "It was Dad's. Mom works in another room now."

Felicity sat in the big leather chair, waiting for Beau to leave. She wanted him out of earshot while she made this call. Once he'd left she dialed Scotty's home number from memory.

"'Lo?" Scotty sounded muzzy with sleep.

"Scotty." Felicity couldn't keep the excitment out of her voice. "I've found the perfect location for the resort."

"I know." Scotty yawned loudly. "That's why you flew out there, remember?"

"Not the ranch," Felicity said impatiently. "It's too rugged—all sagebrush and hay fields. But—"

"What about the ranch house?" Scotty interrupted. "Too run-down to be a dude ranch? Remember, we've already got a buyer willing to pay big bucks."

"It's not run-down," she said. "In fact, it's absolutely beautiful. But it's not for sale. The owners aren't all in agreement, remember? Beau . . . Mr. DuBois is dead set against it. He'll never change his mind."

"Then why the devil did they get you out there?" Scotty sounded wide-awake now.

"You're not listening, Scotty." Felicity picked up a pencil and began tapping it against the blotter. "I called to tell you about the lake. It's ideal. True virgin land. There's nothing like it back East. We could do a really unique resort. It's far enough from the house that we won't be breathing down the family's necks. It'll be better if he, um, *they* don't have to watch the 'dozers roll in.''

"What about this guy who doesn't want to sell?" Scotty asked. "Is he in favor of the lake deal?"

Felicity hesitated. "Not exactly."

Scotty snorted. "What happened to your famous persuasive abilities, kiddo? Haven't you been working on him?"

Felicity flushed. Working on Beau? Beau had been working on *her*. But she couldn't let Scotty know that. "Oh, I'm not concerned," she said airily, wishing she felt as confident as she sounded. "He's stubborn, but I can handle him. When I get through with him, he'll think developing the lake was his idea."

A low growl brought Felicity's eyes up, and they widened in horror. Beau stood in the doorway, his eyes narrowed to slits, his lips tightly compressed. Her stomach lurched as she wondered how much he'd heard. Suddenly she was deeply ashamed of herself. How could she brag about "handling" a man like Beau?

"Attagirl." Scotty's voice fell on her almost deaf ears. "I've never seen a customer resist after you made up your mind."

Felicity couldn't tear her gaze from Beau. "There's always a first time," she murmured. "Look, Scotty, I just wanted to know how high we should go for..." Her words drifted to a halt at the look of betrayal on Beau's angry face.

"Whatever you think, kiddo." Scotty's enthusiasm was undimmed. "You're seeing the place, so I'll rely on your judgment. You still coming home next week?"

Felicity swallowed. "Maybe sooner."

As she replaced the receiver, Beau crossed the room in two strides. With his fists on the desk, he leaned toward her, his eyes glittering furiously.

"Won't have any trouble with me, huh?" His lips curled into the pretense of a grin. "Want to bet on that, Miss Walden?" He turned on his heel and strode out of the office.

Felicity rested her chin on her hand and stared after him. What chance did she have now to convince him of *anything*? In disgust, Felicity threw the pencil across the room at the place where Beau had stood. Oh, why hadn't Scotty handled this deal himself!

CHAPTER SIX

THE NEXT MORNING Felicity breakfasted alone. Wondering if Beau was trying to avoid her, she went outside to look for him. She had to make him realize her solution to his family's dilemma could make everyone happy. Even him, if only he'd bend a little.

Felicity found Ash and Chick Hollings, the ranch foreman, leaning against a corral fence watching Beau work with a skittish red horse. Even from a distance, she could hear the horse snorting angrily as he jumped sideways around the corral. Beau followed slowly, holding a rope attached to the horse's bridle.

"Wouldn't get me on that animal's back," Felicity heard Ash comment as she approached.

She glanced into the corral. Beau wasn't going to *ride* that horse, was he?

Chick nodded in agreement. "Don't know why Beau's pushing him so hard."

"You know Beau."

"Stubborn."

"Who?" Felicity asked their backs. "Beau or the horse?"

Ash spun around. "Morning, Felicity." He gave a short laugh. "Stick around. We're about to find out which one's the stubbornest."

"When it comes to stubborn," muttered the ranch foreman, "I'd put my money on Beau any day."

Felicity nodded vaguely, her anxious eyes still on Beau and the rebellious horse. Any second, the animal could rear up and—

Ash seemed to hear her thoughts. "Beau won't geld this colt. That makes breaking him tougher."

"He acts so wild." Felicity gripped the top rail of the fence, feeling the rough wood dig into her palm. "Why not geld him?"

"Dad gave him to Beau for a birthday present. His sire was the number-one quarter horse in the country and Dad hoped the colt would be a stud horse on our ranch." Ash's eyes returned to the corral. "Breeding him means a lot to Beau."

Felicity's gaze followed his. The colt hadn't settled down at all. He danced away from Beau, his ears flat against his head.

"He shouldn't try to ride him now, should he? Look! He's bucking!" Felicity jumped back from the fence as Beau and the excited colt came near. "He'll throw Beau off."

Ash nodded. "Right. The only question is how often."

Felicity held her breath as she watched Beau pull the horse's head around, slap the saddle a few times and mount. When the animal felt Beau's weight on his back, he began to buck in earnest, pulling his head down and throwing his back up as he leaped again and again into the air. Beau's body whipped back and forth until Felicity thought his neck would break.

"Beau!" she shrieked as he went flying through the air and landed on his back in the dust. Her heart pounding, Felicity started to climb the fence. "Are you all right?"

Beau got slowly to his feet. He leaned over, his breath coming in shallow gasps. "Get off the fence," he croaked.

Felicity hesitated, glancing at the colt, now standing innocently still. She swung her leg over the fence.

"Ash!" Beau rasped. "Get her out of here."

Ash took Felicity's arm and pulled her off the fence. She shook herself loose and glared at Beau. Still breathing hard, he picked up his hat, slapped the dirt off his jeans and walked slowly after the colt. The horse backed away and snorted, pawing the dirt. With her heart in her throat, Felicity watched Beau remount.

"You must be crazy!" she cried as he left the saddle again.

As he hit the dirt, Beau tucked his head under and rolled. Without needing to catch his breath, he stood and walked back to the colt. Felicity realized Beau was going to mount a third time, and she wanted to scream.

She put a hand on Ash's arm. "Isn't there an easier way?"

"You bet," Ash replied. "But Beau always starts 'em this way."

"Ground gettin' pretty hard, Beau?" Chick called, grinning, then muttered under his breath to Ash, "Bet it ain't doin' much for his foul mood, either."

Felicity turned back to the corral, feeling her teeth clench and her fingers curl into fists. Gradually, the tension left her. Though he was still being whipped around by the wayward animal, Beau would obviously stay on this time. It seemed an eternity until the colt began to tire. At last he stood still, his chest heaving in and out. Beau urged him forward, and the horse walked slowly toward them.

Dismounting, Beau handed Chick the reins. "Treat him gently."

Her insides still shaking, Felicity glared at Beau. "Chick was right about you."

"Yeah?" Beau's mouth quirked. "What'd he say?"

"When it comes to stubborn, you're the king."

Beau's eyes glinted. "You'd better believe it, Easterner."

Felicity stared after him as he walked toward the house, his gait unhurried and loose. She could hardly believe he'd just been thrown—twice!—from a horse.

And what did he mean about being so stubborn? That he'd never change his mind about the lake? *That mule-headed cowboy,* she thought grimly. *If he thinks I'm as easy to push around as a two-year-old horse, he's got another think coming!*

Irritation rapidly replaced her fear. Felicity ran after Beau and caught up with him as he was entering his room. Shoving the door open behind him, Felicity followed.

Beau spun around. "Something I can do for you?"

"You're still angry about the phone call."

A thin smile appeared on his lips. "Very perceptive, Miss Walden."

"That's silly," Felicity said. "I came out here to find a place to build a resort. I found it and I was excited. What's wrong with that?"

"Not a thing." Sarcasm dripped from his voice. "Just don't expect to 'handle' me into going along."

"I...ah..." A flush warmed her cheeks. "I shouldn't have said that. But that's no reason for you to take your temper out on that horse."

"Take it out on my horse?" Beau looked shocked. "What are you talking about?"

Felicity hesitated. "Chick said you were in a temper..."

"Chick said!" Beau snorted. "Chick and I disagree about the way to break a horse, that's all." He walked toward the window. "Felicity, I'd never take my temper out on an animal. When I break a horse, I want him honest. I *want* him to buck so he'll learn bucking won't ever do him any good."

"But he bucked you off," Felicity exclaimed. "You could have been hurt."

Beau whirled around, his expression fierce. "I could get hurt a damn sight worse if I got bucked off when I didn't expect it," he growled, slashing his palm through the air.

Felicity took a step back. She'd never seen him so furious. And yet there was a deep sadness in his eyes that tore her heart.

"Beau." She stretched a hand toward him. "What's wrong?"

"Nothing." He folded his arms across his chest. The muscles in his face tightened, hiding any emotion.

Risking his curt dismissal, Felicity moved toward him and touched one arm. She felt sure not all this anger was because of her. "I'm not leaving till you tell me what's the matter," she said with soft insistence.

He stared at her for a moment, then gave a short mirthless laugh. "Okay, stay. I got a little dusty out there. You won't mind if I shower?"

Without another word, Beau unbuttoned his shirt and tugged it out of his jeans. Felicity stood her ground until he reached for the snap in his waistband. Blushing to the roots of her hair, she fled.

Felicity did not see Beau again until dinner. He joined them late and took the chair next to hers, without even a glance in her direction.

"Bud Bonner just called," Beau said to Ash. "The darn fool wants to move a couple hundred head up to his summer pasture."

"What!" Ashley dropped his fork, obviously startled. "It's only May. Is he crazy?"

"You know Bud." Beau helped himself to salad. "Once he makes up his mind, nothing changes it. Says he knows all the signs and spring's early this year. Truth is, I think he's almost out of hay."

"So?" Ash said reasonably. "Why don't we give him some?"

"Believe me, Ash, I tried." Beau shook his head. "He must have felt like a charity case, because he was having none of it. You know his pride."

"Why'd he call then?" Ash poured wine into Cherry's glass.

"Wants us to help with the drive tomorrow," said Beau. "His boys are still down in Laramie at the university. Naturally I said we'd help."

Ash slapped the table angrily. "Beau, it's crazy to move his herd up there this early! There's always some kind of storm in May. We'll be responsible if those animals starve." He jabbed the air wildly with his fork.

"Ash, it's for Bud," Beau said, his dark eyes flashing. "I said we'd help. Right?"

Though Beau's demanding tone and fierce glare were not directed at her, Felicity felt the force of them. She wasn't surprised when Ash gave in.

"Right," he grumbled and went back to filling his plate from the platter of trout.

"Bud Bonner once saved my husband's life," Alma explained to Felicity. "They were very close."

She smiled at the older woman, relieved someone at the table was still speaking to her.

"Hey, Felicity," Ash said suddenly. "Why don't you ride along with us tomorrow? It's real pretty country."

"Well...um...." Felicity stalled for time.

"Ride along?" Beau snapped. "In what? The pickup? She can't ride a horse."

Nettled, Felicity spoke without thinking. "I can, too."

Beau turned to her, a brow raised ironically. "Yeah? What have you ridden—a merry-go-round?"

Her foot tapped furiously under the table. "I used to rent horses all summer when I was a kid." She gulped, wondering what she was getting herself into. "It's been a few years, but I'm sure I can still ride...." Felicity remembered the colt Beau had ridden that morning. "You do have a gentle horse, don't you?"

"Not gentle enough for a dude," said Beau.

"Sure we do," said Ash. "You'll love her."

Beau frowned at his brother. "Lolo?"

"Of course, Lolo." Ash turned back to Felicity. "We got her for Cherry to learn to ride."

"No thanks. Not me." Cherry held up her hands. "Are you sure you want to do this, Felicity? You'll be on that horse forever."

"How long will it be?" Felicity asked, beginning to regret her hasty words.

"We'll start from Bud's place about sunup," Ash said.

"She'll never make it all day." Beau interrupted. He glanced at Felicity. "You'd better just meet us at the end of our road about noon."

"It's the scenery above here that's worth seeing," agreed Ash. "It's not a bad ride. Only one steep grade."

"Nothing you can't *handle* though, right, Felicity?"

Felicity couldn't miss the irony in Beau's voice, nor the smirk on his lips. Clenching her fists in her lap, she returned his challenging stare. "I use an English saddle," she said primly. "I hope you have one."

Beau shook his head. "Wouldn't be caught dead with one."

Ash seemed to feel none of the tension sparking between Felicity and Beau. "Sure we do, Beau. We've got that old one Gramma always used."

Beau spoke through clenched teeth. "Gramma didn't come on cattle drives." He gave Felicity a stern look. "Lolo's a cow pony. You'll have to use a Western saddle."

For some reason, Felicity felt Beau was testing her and her Eastern ideas. Besides, she was sick of being bossed around by him. "No thanks," she said firmly. "I'll use the English."

Beau folded his forearms on the table and glared at her. Deep in his blue eyes, Felicity saw a glint of amusement. Slowly the little half smile softened his lips. "Okay, Easterner," he said grudgingly. "I'll tell Chick."

After dinner the men turned in early to be up for the cattle drive, but Felicity didn't feel a bit sleepy. Most nights since she'd arrived, she and Beau had stayed up, comparing Florida to Wyoming, ranching to real estate, East to

West. She realized now that their friendly conversations had only been another of Beau's attempts to wear her down, but she'd enjoyed them anyway. With a sigh, she decided to work on her proposal in front of the fire.

When Felicity returned from her room with her arms full of papers, she found Beau, wearing a short navy-blue robe, bent over the hearth poking the fire. The sight of his muscular thighs, covered with dark curly hair, unsettled her. She looked quickly away as he straightened.

"I hope you don't mind if I work here," she said in a strained voice, trying to remember exactly what she'd been planning to do.

"Work away." Beau sat down on the love seat and stretched out a bare leg on the coffee table. "Don't let me bother you."

Bother me? Felicity thought dazedly, her gaze traveling up his leg to the hem of his robe. For days she'd resisted the pull of Beau's rough masculinity. Since their trip to the lake, it had become impossible to ignore. Now it threatened to overwhelm her. She swallowed hard, knowing how foolish she'd look if she just ran out of the room.

She forced herself to sound natural. "Of course you bother me. You're the only problem I have here." Flipping open a file, she dug out a map of the lake.

The half smile tugged at Beau's lips. "Don't, Felicity."

She ignored the fluttery feeling that stole over her. "Don't what?"

He sat up and pulled the map out of her hands. "Don't work."

"That's why I'm here, Beau."

He returned the map to her file and closed it. "Take a night off. You work too hard anyway."

With the map out of her hands, Felicity had no excuse to keep her eyes lowered. As her gaze met Beau's, the rush of attraction hit her again like a sledgehammer.

"I'd better go to bed," she murmured.

"It's too early," he said. "I couldn't sleep, either. Let's talk awhile."

Felicity looked away from Beau's leg on the coffee table, but her attention was caught by the teasing grin deepening the corners of his mouth. His lips, usually so firm, looked softer tonight, more sensuous.

Her lungs didn't seem to be working properly. She opened her lips to take in more air. *What's happening to me?* she wondered helplessly. Her struggle to control the sensations Beau's near-nudity aroused in her was shattering her composure. And she had an uneasy feeling he knew it.

She jumped up. "I can't, Beau." Her voice cracked. "You've got hardly anything on." Wincing at her foolish words, she spun around to leave.

"Don't run away, Felicity. I'm not going to bite you," he teased, his voice gentle. "And I promise not to take off my robe."

Now he was laughing at her. Steeling herself, Felicity raised her eyes. "You'll just get angry again, like this morning."

"I was kind of angry, wasn't I?" He lifted a shoulder. "We don't see eye to eye about the ranch—yet."

Felicity looked suspiciously at his laughing blue eyes. "What do you mean 'yet'?"

"Let's talk about something else." Beau tugged her back toward the love seat.

Felicity looked at the narrow seat, felt his warm hands holding hers— She had to get out of there! "Beau, please." Her voice wavered. "I ought to go to bed."

Beau moved his hands up her arms to her shoulders, sending sparks along her nerves. Her mouth opened, but the words of protest stuck in her throat as Beau's arm slid down her back and encircled her waist.

"Okay, I'll walk you to your room."

In the narrow hallway their bodies were pressed together. Felicity tried to pull away, but Beau held her tight. When they reached her door, he turned her toward him. He stroked a finger down her cheek, curled it under her chin and tilted her face up to his. When their eyes met, a fire kindled in Felicity. Beau's eyes darkened with desire. *I can't let this happen,* she thought wildly, unable to move.

His full lips softened under her helpless gaze, making her fingertips tingle with the need to touch them. She sensed Beau was going to kiss her. Her mind shrieked at her to stop him. But she couldn't stop herself.

His mouth brushed hers, tasting her with light nips before gently forcing open her lips, sending a bolt of desire through her. Felicity wrapped her arms around Beau's neck and buried her fingers in his curly hair. His hands moved to her waist and pulled her closer, and Felicity's bones seemed to melt. Beau's lips trailed kisses down her neck. As her head tipped back into his caressing hand she gave a soft moan.

Suddenly Felicity knew she had to stop this *now*. Part of her wanted it to go on and on, wanted Beau to lift her in his arms and carry her to her room, wanted to be closer and closer to him until... Somehow she found the strength to move her hands between them and push hard, against his heaving chest.

"Beau...please...stop," she begged, trembling. "I can't...we can't..."

She buried her face in his shoulder. Beau held her, tenderly stroking her hair, while Felicity leaned against him, letting her breathing quiet.

"If this is how you plan to handle me," Beau said at last, "I think I'm going to like it."

"Handle *you*?" Felicity said, shocked. "You kissed *me*, not the other way around."

She felt Beau's chuckle rumble in his chest. "You can't be serious."

"Want to bet?"

Tunneling his fingers into her tight chignon, Beau gently tugged till he looked into her wide green eyes. A smile creased his face. "You sure looked like a woman who wanted to be kissed, Felicity."

Felicity quickly lowered her lashes. Had she asked for his kisses? She hadn't meant to, yet here she was still wrapped deliciously in his arms. Her mind churned with confusion.

"Beau." She tried to pull away. "We shouldn't do this. It's not ... it's not businesslike."

Beau's body shook with laughter. "No, Miss Walden, it sure isn't. It's one hell of an improvement on business. But you're right." Expelling a deep breath, he released her. "I should keep my hands to myself. You'll agree even more tomorrow."

"What do you mean?" Without his strong arms around her, Felicity felt cold.

"After six hours on a horse, your body will tell you what you won't listen to from me. You don't belong out here." The twinkle faded from his dark eyes. "Neither does your resort."

"Oh, Beau, you're the one who won't listen!" She whirled away and darted into her room.

As Felicity snuggled into her soft bed, thoughts of Beau went round and round in her head. What was he doing to her? Was this just a new tactic? No, she didn't believe that. His kisses had been too passionate, his desire too evident.

With a blush hidden by the darkness, she touched her fingertips to lips still swollen and quivering from Beau's demanding touch. Did he know how much she had liked kissing him? Could he tell she'd almost ... almost what? Felicity sat up. She hadn't almost anything, and she hoped Beau knew that!

It wouldn't happen again, she vowed, smacking a fist into her palm. From now on she would not be alone with Beau under any circumstances. If she took care, she ought to be able to finish this job without another incident like tonight's. Felicity tossed uneasily, wondering if that was really what she wanted.

CHAPTER SEVEN

THE FOLLOWING MORNING Felicity woke before dawn, too keyed-up about the cattle drive—and Beau—to go back to sleep. A long hot soak, she decided, was what she needed to relax. Before she climbed out of the claw-footed tub, sunlight streamed through the window and the water had grown tepid.

Usually a speedy dresser, Felicity stalled over her choice of footwear. Her only possibilities were sneakers or navy suede boots with a matching vest. Either would look ridiculous on a cattle drive. With an inward groan, she finally chose the boots. Though she wasn't working today, she twisted her hair into her usual chignon. The more businesslike she felt around Beau, the better.

Long past sunup, when she was sure the men would be gone, Felicity wandered out to the dining room, only to find the very situation she had resolved to avoid: she was alone with Beau. He stood by the table in his stocking feet, fastening the snaps on his chambray shirt with one hand while he forked down eggs with the other.

"Morning, Felicity," he said, gulping coffee.

In spite of herself, Felicity felt a rush of pleasure at seeing him. "I thought you'd be long gone by now."

"Ash left ages ago." Beau bent down to pull on a worn cowboy boot. "I overslept."

The disgruntled look on his face made Felicity laugh. "How could you sleep late on such a beautiful day?"

"You might well ask," he replied, "since it's your fault."

"My fault! What did I do?"

Beau gave her a curious look. "You left me in no condition to sleep, Felicity. I suppose you nodded right off, while I tossed and turned all night."

Color rushed to Felicity's cheeks. She turned away and poured a cup of coffee to cover her embarrassment. But she couldn't just ignore this. She had to make Beau understand that last night was an isolated incident and that it would not be repeated.

"To tell you the truth," she said crisply, "I slept like a log."

"Great." Beau sounded as if he meant it. "I'd hate to see you miss the cattle drive."

"Miss the cattle drive?" Felicity said, surprised. "You thought I'd sleep that late?"

"I thought you might avoid . . . Never mind." Beau took a last swig of coffee. "When you're ready, just find Chick. I told him to saddle Lolo for you."

Felicity nodded halfheartedly, nervous once again about getting on a horse after all this time.

Beau stopped with his hand on the mudroom door. "You don't have to come if you're scared."

Felicity flinched. "I'm not scared, Beau. I just . . ."

"There's really nothing to worry about," he assured her. "Lolo's dude-proof."

Felicity pursed her lips. "You just want to show me how beautiful your mountains are without condos."

Beau looked as though he intended to deny it, then he shrugged and grinned. "True," he admitted. "But if you decide to stay home, I'll understand."

Felicity's business acumen told her that if she backed down now, Beau would never take her seriously. "I'll be there at noon," she said firmly.

"Good." Beau's lips twitched as he glanced at her boots. "Why don't you borrow a pair of real boots from the mudroom? You'll be a lot more comfortable." He shook his head as he eyed the rest of her outfit—suede vest, powder-blue jersey and pleated jeans—but he refrained from comment.

Felicity opened her mouth to tell him she hadn't bought a whole Western wardrobe for this trip, but he was out the door before she could speak.

A few hours later, Felicity donned the snakeskin cowboy boots Alma had given her and went to find Chick. She hurried in and out of several buildings before she found him grooming an enormous golden horse in one of the corrals.

Felicity approached cautiously. "What in the world is that?"

"A Belgian workhorse." Chick looked up from running a stiff brush down the horse's massive leg. "Sometimes in the winter we still feed using these ol' boys and a sled. Beau keeps three teams for winter storms." He slapped the horse's behind, and the huge animal trotted away.

"Thank heavens," Felicity said with relief. "I thought that was Lolo."

"Lolo?" Laughing heartily, Chick led her into a barn to a much smaller gray horse with spotted hindquarters. "Here's Lolo. She's part Tennessee Walker. Give you a real smooth ride."

Once on Lolo's back, Felicity felt right at home. Her anxiety about the ride began to dissolve as she and Lolo galloped down the DuBois ranch road. Long before she saw them, Felicity heard the bellowing of cattle. When she reached the highway, she jerked her horse to a halt.

Hundreds of cows covered the road, their eyes wide, their bellows deafening, as they moved, seemingly under protest, at the urging of the cowboys and two well-trained dogs. Up close, these nervous cows looked a lot larger than the placid creatures she'd seen grazing Beau's pastures. It was hard to believe a handful of riders could control such a sea of animals.

Felicity looked anxiously around for Beau. Astride a large bay stallion, he was moving cows out of the path of a car working its way through the herd.

A cow darted past her, and Lolo pranced back and forth in her eagerness to chase it. Felicity clung to the reins as she stared at Beau, hoping he would join her behind the herd. At last he noticed her and waved as he began threading his way through the milling cattle to her side.

Though she was relieved to have Beau riding beside her, she tried to hide her nervousness. "Who are the others on horseback?" she asked with forced calm.

"That's Bud Bonner," Beau said, pointing at a barrel-chested man with white hair. "The girl is Bud's daughter, Bobby Jo. Rides real well, doesn't she? This must be about the millionth cattle drive we've been on together."

Felicity felt a stab of jealousy at the admiration in Beau's voice as her gaze followed his to the tall brunette whose wide brown eyes were shaded by a white cowboy hat. Her athletic body moved in perfect unison with her pinto pony. Felicity suddenly felt very very Eastern. Her thighs tensed as Lolo followed Beau's horse toward the herd.

"If you're going to ride this close, Felicity," Beau cautioned, "keep alert."

Felicity refrained from telling Beau that she hadn't chosen to ride this close, Lolo had.

"If a cow rushes you," he continued, "yip at it and wave your arms."

These instructions did nothing to improve Felicity's already shaky confidence. She'd feel a perfect fool shouting "yip yip yip" at a cow. Yet there, a few feet away and looking appealingly feminine in her Levi's and cowboy shirt, was another woman doing a real job just as well as the men. Felicity wished she'd never left Tampa.

When Bobby Jo rode to the back of the herd, Beau introduced her. A moment later, he galloped off after a lagging calf, and Felicity followed Bobby Jo. As they approached the thick of the herd, cows shoved against Lo-lo's legs, making Felicity as tense as her horse.

"Bobby Jo," she shouted over the bellows of the close-packed cattle, "how can we take up the whole highway this way?"

"It's okay as long as—yip yip—we have flagmen ahead and behind. But we have to get them off the road as soon as we can." Bobby Jo flapped her arms. "Yip whoop whoop!"

At every yip, Lolo skittered and stretched her neck toward the herd. Felicity's fingers ached from gripping the reins.

"Can I ask you a question?" said Bobby Jo.

"I guess so," Felicity said nervously, wondering how to control her cow pony so close to the cattle.

"Why do you want to bust up the DuBois ranch when they all love it so?" Bobby Jo took her eyes off the cows only long enough to scowl at Felicity.

Felicity hesitated. Obviously, Bobby Jo had waited until Beau wasn't around to ask her this, and Felicity didn't know how much he'd told Bobby Jo. It wasn't Felicity's place to reveal family secrets. Besides, she couldn't have a serious discussion with someone who kept yipping at cows.

She shrugged. "I didn't call them, Bobby Jo. They called me."

"Well, I think land profiteering is an awful way to make a living," Bobby Jo sneered. "It'll destroy Beau to lose his ranch. You must be pretty heartless." With that, Bobby Jo kicked her horse and rode off yipping loudly.

Openmouthed, Felicity stared after her, shocked at the woman's rudeness. When she had once more pulled Lolo behind the teeming cattle, her pulse began to slow and Felicity wondered about Bobby Jo's choice of words. "Land profiteering" sounded like something Beau would say.

During the next few hours, Felicity stayed at the rear of the herd, but her eyes were drawn repeatedly to Beau. On the back of a horse, working cattle, he was in his element—

his every move exuded the natural confidence of a man doing what he loved and doing it well. Felicity had never thought him weak; she would have been a fool if she had. But now, watching him use the power of his body to control his horse and the cows, Felicity suddenly knew she'd underestimated his strength. A fierce tug of attraction made her jerk her gaze back to the mountains. She'd got into enough trouble last night; she certainly didn't want to invite more.

Finally, Beau rode over to her, one hand on the reins, the other resting on his thigh. He looked so relaxed that Felicity, whose back was beginning to ache, envied him.

"Wait here, till we get the cows off the road," he said. "We have to get them through a narrow gate, and it makes them nervous."

Felicity slowed her horse and looked around the deep valley. On her right, in a large field backed by towering mountains, was a herd of beautiful pronghorn antelope. As the dogs and men maneuvered the lowing cattle through the gate, the antelope took to their heels, gracefully leaping fallen logs and underbrush as they ran.

Felicity followed the cows through the gate. Suddenly she heard a loud cracking noise and saw a flash of yellow.

Lolo bolted.

As her horse lurched Felicity rocked in the saddle and grasped helplessly at the reins. But it was too late. Lolo was gone, and Felicity felt herself falling. She landed painfully in the grass, all the air whooshing from her lungs.

Before she could inhale a much needed breath, Beau was beside her. His strong hands gripped her upper arms. "Are you all right?" His dark eyes searched her face.

"Felicity!" He gave her a shake. "Talk to me."

As the pain in her bottom slowly eased, Felicity tried to draw breath into her tortured lungs. "If you make one single remark about dudes, Beau DuBois," she croaked at last, "I'll punch you right in the nose."

Relief melted Beau's features. "I guess you're all right. Your tongue's working fine."

Taking his outstretched hand, Felicity got stiffly to her feet. She winced as he brushed grass from the seat of her jeans.

"What happened?" she asked, still gripping Beau's hand. "What was that noise?"

"Bobby Jo flicked her slicker at you." Beau's voice roughened with anger. "It's sort of an initiation for dudes. Some cowboys think it's funny—some cowgirls, too." Beau frowned at Felicity. "Of course, if you hadn't been using that stupid flat saddle, you'd have stayed on."

Felicity dropped his hand. Why was he yelling at her? Before she could think of a suitably crushing response, Bobby Jo rode up, leading Lolo and grinning broadly.

Beau glared at her, "Not funny, Bobby Jo." His voice shook with anger. "You know how I feel about that trick."

Bobby Jo's grin faded. "Well, *she* deserves it if anyone does."

"The hell she does!" Beau shouted, slapping his cowboy hat against his thigh. "I'm responsible for Miss Walden on this drive. If you—"

"Hah." Bobby Jo wheeled her horse and galloped away.

"Grow up, Bobby Jo," Beau growled. "C'mon, Felicity, I'll give you a leg up."

Every muscle in Felicity's body protested as she straddled her horse. She had much preferred the feel of solid ground beneath her feet and Beau's supporting hand around hers—at least until he'd started lecturing her. But she didn't want anyone, especially Bobby Jo, to think she was scared. Ignoring her aches and her nervousness, she kicked Lolo lightly and started up the mountain after the others.

When they reached Bud's pasture, Felicity had to catch her breath again. No wonder Beau had asked her to come. The pasture was on a ridge overlooking a vast, unspoiled valley that rolled away for miles. Thick stands of dark pine and golden-green quaking aspen contrasted with the lush grass of the meadows. A sparkling alpine stream, dammed here and there by beavers, meandered across the valley. Range upon range of towering snowcapped peaks surrounded it all.

As she gazed at the view, Felicity had a glimpse at last of how Beau must feel about his land. This beautiful untouched valley was a treasure, protected from man for centuries by the impassable mountains that enclosed it. Though she couldn't have put it into words, Felicity knew something inside her had changed forever.

Beau and Ash rode up then. When they, too, stopped to stare at the land they loved, Felicity realized this sight could never grow old.

Beau finally broke the silence. "Now can I say 'I told you so'?"

Felicity shook her head. "Don't bother," she said. "I . . . Don't talk at all."

Beau's eyes filled with understanding. "I wondered if I'd ever see you run out of words."

Felicity couldn't drag her gaze away from the vista before her. "I think my whole memory of Wyoming will start over from this moment."

"You have the right instincts, Easterner. You're just in the wrong job."

Bobby Jo rode up behind them. "Hadn't we better start back, Beau?"

Beau called his dogs and went to tell Bud they were ready to go. Felicity sat looking over the valley with Ash.

"I don't see how I can leave this," Ash said, waving an arm to encompass the valley. "I told myself all morning to stay in the pasture, away from the ridge. But I couldn't. We came here with Dad, you know, every summer. How can I leave it forever?" He looked up to watch a hawk soaring effortlessly on the wind currents.

"The way Cherry feels," Felicity said, as the bird suddenly pulled in its wings and dived toward the earth, "how can you stay?"

Ash shrugged his shoulders helplessly. "We can't, I guess."

The hawk rose skyward with a small rodent in its talons. Felicity shivered. The easy grace of the big bird had blinded her to its ruthlessness as a hunter.

Felicity turned to face Ash, feeling a strong wave of compassion for him. Though her lake development might be the answer for Beau and Alma, Ash would remain in the middle—caught between his love for his Eastern wife and for his Western way of life.

"Couldn't Cherry ever feel at home here?"

"Not likely." Ash shook his head resignedly. "You'd have to see Cherry in the winter to understand. She's a different person."

"Hey, you two," Beau called, waving his hat, "are you coming?"

As they set off down the mountain, a weary silence settled over them. Yet the peace of the valley stayed with Felicity. Beau was right. Such a place should never be developed. But her resort wouldn't be anywhere near it. She wouldn't despoil it in any way.

As the highway stretched ahead of them, Felicity thought her saddle had turned to concrete. Her body throbbed with every step of the horse. She leaned forward to stroke Lolo's neck and take the weight off her aching hips. Closing her eyes, Felicity simply let the mare follow the others, wondering if the ranch house would ever appear.

Chick was waiting in the yard to take the horses. Felicity was so stiff she almost fell out of the saddle. When she took a few steps toward the house, her legs started to give way; she felt completely numb below the waist.

Just in time, Beau came up behind her and slipped his arm around her. "You Easterners," he teased, "do everything too fast. When you haven't been on a horse for ten years, don't just hop off and start running. Take it easy."

Gratefully, Felicity leaned against his chest, inhaling his rugged male scent, a mixture of sweat and cows. "I'm not running," she admitted. "I'm falling. My legs won't do what I tell them."

Contact with Beau's body was sending dangerous currents of pleasure through her stiff limbs, but she had no desire to pull away. She needed Beau's strength for support.

"You'll be good as new after half an hour in the hot tub." His neutral tone did nothing to slow Felicity's heart rate. "Did you bring a swimsuit?"

Trying to ignore her hopelessly inappropriate response to his touch, Felicity grasped Beau's shoulder and rubbed first one thigh then the other in an effort to bring them back to life.

"Of course," she answered, managing a grin. "Floridians take bathing suits everywhere."

"Then I'll join you in the tub."

Beau's eyes followed her hand as it moved over her hips. Embarrassed, Felicity stopped her massage and tried to support her own weight.

"Think you can walk now?" he asked.

"Yes, I'm fine." Felicity looked away, not wanting Beau to see how she was reacting to him. "I was just a little stiff at first."

A sigh escaped her as Beau's arm left her waist. Maintaining a businesslike relationship would be a lot easier if Beau would keep his hands to himself.

Felicity glanced up at him. With his cowboy hat pushed back on his head, his curly hair falling across his brow and his open, concerned expression, Beau was the picture of Western sincerity. But Felicity didn't believe it for a second.

Without his strong arm distracting her, Felicity realized with a jolt that this whole day was simply another of Beau's tricks. Bobby Jo's expertise, the unspoiled valley, her aching muscles, had all been carefully orchestrated to make her feel out of her element. And she'd almost fallen for it!

Nice try, Beau, you sneak, she thought, narrowing her eyes at his boyish grin.

But even that beautiful valley wouldn't make Felicity forget her job. Her lake resort wouldn't ruin his precious valley. Beau could ride up and look at it any time he wanted. And it wouldn't kill him to share it.

Felicity smiled sweetly, echoing Beau's innocent expression. "See you in the hot tub," she said and walked into the house.

CHAPTER EIGHT

FELICITY WINCED as she pulled her white bathing suit over her bruised hips. An uneasy glance at her reflection almost made her wince again. The neckline, if it could be called that, plunged below her navel, and the tiny purple and turquoise strips that held the suit together left a lot of skin exposed. After vowing not to be alone with Beau, what had possessed her to agree to this? Just the two of them—together in the hot tub? She must be nuts!

But as she clipped her long hair into a knot on top of her head, and imagined that warm bubbly water soothing her aching body, she couldn't bear to pass it up. Slipping on a terry robe, she made her way out to the deck, determined to remain businesslike and composed even in the tub.

As she entered the glass enclosure, Beau turned from starting the air jets. His black fitted swim trunks hid little of his hard lean body. Felicity fought a sudden desire to touch the thick curly hair that covered his chest. Swallowing hard, she looked down and tugged at her zipper. When she stepped out of her robe, she heard Beau suck in his breath. "That's a nasty bruise," he said through clenched teeth.

Felicity looked at him curiously. Why should *he* be so upset? she wondered. She was the one with the sore bottom. "I'll live."

Beau glared at her for a moment, a muscle twitching in his jaw. Finally, with an obvious effort, he relaxed and offered her his hand to help her down the slippery steps. "If you sit over here, Felicity, you can see the mountains."

Holding tight to his strong hand, Felicity eased herself into the hot water with a sigh of pleasure and gingerly sat down. Her breasts stirred gently as the bubbling water began to soothe away her aches and tensions. The lowering sun colored the fir-clad mountains a pinky gold. Releasing Beau's hand, Felicity leaned her head back against the rim of the hot tub and looked up to see the evening star sparkling above her.

"I must be in heaven," she sighed.

"It just looks like heaven." Beau sat across from her in front of an air jet, letting the water bubble around his shoulders. "I'll be enjoying that view for years to come. Tonight it's all yours."

Felicity made a face at him. "Is that a hint?"

"Yep, sure is."

"You haven't even heard my ideas yet." Felicity chewed her lip in irritation. "I didn't really want to talk business tonight, but—"

"Then don't." Beau stretched his arms along the edge of the tub. "My mind's made up anyway. I learned my lesson last fall."

"You stubborn cowboy!" Felicity exclaimed, slapping the water. "You don't even know what I'm going to say. It wouldn't hurt you to listen. I have a solution—a way you can all have what you want."

Beau's lips curled cynically. "You mean a way you can have what *you* want."

"Just listen, would you?" With an effort, Felicity softened her voice. She knew this was hard for Beau. "Why not sell us just the lake and forest around it? Of course, we'd need a right-of-way, but it wouldn't have to come anywhere near your home. You could keep the ranch and have enough money to buy Ash out."

"And you'd put condos all around my lake. There wouldn't be a trout left for miles. No thanks." Beau's voice was calm but emphatic. "Besides, we need that water for irrigation."

"You could keep the water rights, Beau." Felicity shifted in the warm tub, and her wriggling toes accidentally bumped Beau's. The contact reminded her that she had to keep her mind on business. "Do you think you're the only one who's ever considered the environment?"

Beau gave her a lazy smile. "Look at the mountains for a while. We'll talk business later."

Too tired to argue, Felicity let the lapping water relax her. "You're about as easy to deal with as that moose that charged us."

"Charged us?" Beau laughed. "A charging moose doesn't stop, Easterner. She'd probably been there watching us for quite a while."

Felicity shuddered at the thought.

"But tell your friends in Florida she was charging." Beau's lips twitched into his little half smile. "It'll make a better story."

"Hah," Felicity said. "I don't need to embellish stories about Wyoming to make them more exciting. This place is strange enough all by itself."

Beau smiled knowingly. "I thought you'd feel that way after the cattle drive."

"Did you just say, 'I told you so'?" Felicity asked.

Beau let the smile reach his eyes. "Something like that."

"Well, you're wrong." She wasn't arguing now, just telling him. "Sure I'm tired, and I did feel out of place on the cattle drive. But that's why people take a vacation! To go someplace exotic and do something they'd never get to do at home."

"Oh yeah?" Beau waved his hand dismissively, sending a splash of water in her direction. "And when they get here, the same thing would happen to them as happened to you. What if you'd been alone when you were thrown and couldn't catch your horse? What if you'd broken your leg?"

His hands clenched into fists and he folded his arms across his chest. "Do you know how I felt when I saw Lolo bolt?" His voice roughened. "I *knew* you wouldn't stay on."

"I thought it was part of the plan."

Beau's brows lowered into a straight bushy line. "What's that supposed to mean?"

"You know..." she said hesitantly, surprised by the rage she heard in his voice. "I thought... What you said last night. That after the cattle drive, I'd know I didn't belong here."

Beau stood up in the water and took a step toward her. "You thought," he thundered, "that I would intentionally let a horse throw you?"

Felicity shrank down into the water. Beau towered over her, anger evident in every line of his body. She didn't understand it. He grabbed her wrist and pulled her to her feet.

"Look at this," he yelled, running his finger down her bruised hip and thigh. "You think I had anything to do with this?"

Felicity flinched at his touch and tried to pull away. "Beau, you're hurting me," she protested.

Beau threw her wrist back at her and spun away. Gasping, Felicity stared at his rigid back. Something about those taut muscles, looking like bands of steel between his shoulder blades, made her want to cry. Instinctively she knew Beau's anger, like his anger yesterday morning in his bedroom, went far deeper than this moment. Her irritation with him was forgotten. Felicity saw only that Beau was suffering, and her heart went out to him.

Moving toward him, she put her hands on his shoulders and leaned her cheek against his back. He didn't move.

"Beau," she said quietly. "I'm not really hurt. It's just a bruise."

She felt his chest rise and fall. "If I'd known that spoiled brat, Bobby Jo..." A shudder passed through him. "I should have known. I should never have let you go."

Felicity wanted to shake him. "You couldn't have stopped me. I'm not a child, you know. I make my own decisions."

He turned to her, his face stony. "Not on my ranch, you don't."

The anguished look in his eyes stopped her words of argument. "But I'm fine, Beau."

He gripped her shoulders. "Do you know what could have happened to you?"

She covered his hands with her own, feeling warmth spread through her body. "You fell off your horse yesterday. What's the difference?"

"I expected to be thrown. I was ready for it." He pulled his hands away and stared into the distance, his expression closed. "You can get hurt a lot worse when you don't know it's coming."

Felicity sensed him drawing away from her, but he didn't resist when she urged him to sit down beside her. Taking his hand, she began tracing the lines in his palm with her thumb.

"Beau?" A lump in her throat that she didn't understand made it hard to talk. "What's this all about?"

He glared at her, then looked away. "I don't know what you mean."

"Yes, you do." She continued to massage his palm, her fingers moving up his forearm. "It might help you to talk about it. You can trust me."

He gave her a long measuring look. Gradually the tautness left his jaw, and his shoulders slumped against the rim of the tub. "I guess I believe that," he said at last.

Beau pulled his hand free and pushed the damp hair off his forehead. Twice he opened his mouth to speak before any sound came out.

"My father..." He clenched his jaw. "He died after a fall from a horse. A young gelding, his first time out of the corral. He threw Dad into a tree. Dad...died before we could get help."

Felicity's chest ached at the pain she saw in Beau's eyes. "You were with him?"

Beau nodded. "Chick and I. Chick went for help. I stayed with Dad." Beau swallowed. "He died in my arms."

Felicity bit her lip, holding back tears. She remembered that endless night when her mother had nearly died, remembered how frightened she'd been waiting with her father, praying the doctors would know what to do. How much worse it would have been if she'd been alone with her mother, helpless, unable to save her.

"Was he conscious?" she asked. "Did he know you were with him?"

Beau rubbed his eyes. "He knew he was dying." Beau's voice was thick with emotion. "He told me when I had a son...not to wait until I was dying to tell him I loved him."

Felicity leaned her head against Beau's chest, hiding the tears that flowed down her cheeks. Beau gently stroked her back. Now that he had begun, the words poured out of him.

"I can still hear him," Beau said. "His voice got weaker and weaker as his life seeped away. I kept telling him to rest, to save his strength. But he wouldn't." Beau's hand twisted into her hair, clenching tightly. "He told me how much he loved the ranch, how much it meant to him to be working land his father and grandfathers had loved. He could die in peace, he said, because he knew I felt that way, too. He knew I'd nurture the land as he had—that my sons would grow up the same way, with the same love of ranching."

Felicity couldn't speak. She felt Beau's thumb under her chin turning her face up to his. Gently he brushed the tears from her cheeks.

"I never told Mom or Ash," he continued, pain glittering in his dark eyes. "I would have when I could finally talk about it. But by then, they'd begun to think about selling the ranch, and I couldn't. I knew it would hurt them too much. And why I'm telling a half-pint real estate developer from

Florida—'' his half smile flashed for just a second ''—is beyond me.''

"I'm glad you did, Beau," she murmured, gulping back tears. "I wish I could say something to make it hurt less."

"It hurts less now," he said. "I've needed to talk about it for a long time." He leaned toward her and gave her a gentle kiss on the forehead. "Thanks, Felicity."

Little rushes of pleasure flowed through her as his lips brushed her skin. "I didn't do anything, Beau," she murmured.

Uneasily, she slid a few inches away from him along the bench. She felt so close to him right now, she was afraid their emotions could explode again into the kind of physical intimacy they'd shared last night.

As they sat quietly in the soothing bubbles, Felicity's churning emotions calmed. When Beau finally spoke, he, too, sounded more at ease.

"Do you know what time it is?" he asked.

Felicity looked out at the rosy sky and asked her tired body how long she'd been up. "About a million o'clock?" she suggested.

Beau laughed. "Not quite. But it's almost eight. Dinnertime. Aren't you hungry? Lunch was hours ago."

"Actually, I was so nervous about the cattle drive I forgot to eat lunch. I must be famished, but I hate to get out of this tub." Felicity slid lower in the water. "I think I'll skip dinner."

"You're too tired," said Beau. "You might fall asleep out here alone and drown. It's one of the dangers of a hot tub."

"Don't be silly. I've spent half my life in the ocean. This little hot tub's nothing. But if you're worried, feel free to stay with me."

"I'd like to, but I can't," he replied. "We're all meeting Bud and Bobby Jo in Pinedale later to go dancing. You, too."

"Me?" Felicity's green eyes flashed at Beau. After this afternoon, she had no intention of meeting Bobby Jo anywhere. "I thought you were mad at Bobby Jo. You called her..."

"A spoiled brat?" Beau said, grinning. "That she is, and it's much too late to spank any sense into her. But she and her father are our oldest friends, and when I make a date I keep it."

"You should," replied Felicity. "Just don't expect *me* to keep it. I'll stay right where I am."

"I can't leave you out here, Felicity."

Beau stood up and took a few steps toward her in the waist-deep water. When he held out his hand, she looked up, her gaze momentarily lost in the dark tangle of hair on his chest. She forced her attention back to his face.

Felicity knew Beau was only being sensible. But she hated to leave this luscious hot water just because *he* had a date with Bobby Jo. Not, she assured herself, because she was jealous of Bobby Jo. She didn't think of Beau that way at all. It was just that they'd been so close a moment ago, and now—

Beau took another step toward her.

Well, it certainly wasn't worth arguing about. Pushing past Beau with as much dignity as she could muster, Felicity climbed out of the tub and walked briskly down the hall toward her room.

"Felicity, wait!"

As she reached for the doorknob, Beau's hand closed on her arm. He draped her robe over her shoulders and turned her to face him.

"You forgot your robe, Easterner," he said, pulling it snugly around her. He waited for Felicity to raise her eyes to his. "We always go dancing after cattle drives. It's more of a tradition than a date."

Felicity blushed. Beau didn't owe her an explanation. He could go out with whomever he pleased. "I, um, just don't like being told what to do, Beau," she murmured.

"I've noticed that," he said, the laugh lines crinkling beside his eyes. "Look where it got you this afternoon—right on your you-know-what. If you'd listened to me, you'd have stayed on your horse."

"Just because you were right once," Felicity said defensively, "doesn't mean you always are, you know."

Beau released a long breath. "Let's not argue anymore. I'm too hungry." He cupped her cheek softly for a moment. "Thanks for listening."

"You don't have to thank me, Beau."

He leaned forward to whisper in her ear, his voice full of humor. "And don't forget your date with Bobby Jo."

"Beau DuBois!" Felicity poked him in the chest, feeling silky hair tickle her finger.

His hand covered hers, curling her fingers into a fist. "Don't bother to dress up, Easterner. We're pretty casual here."

Laughing, he let her go and Felicity ducked into her room. That man could try the patience of a saint, she thought, slamming the door behind her. She felt as if her emotions had been tied to a yo-yo for the past hour, with Beau manipulating the string.

After hanging her bathing suit on the side of the tub to dry, Felicity found a pair of pleated linen slacks that fit loosely over her bruises and added a maroon shirt. Her hair was still damp so she left it down, swinging loose. Drying it would take too long. She didn't want to spend any more time alone thinking about Beau.

After dinner, while Cherry dressed to go dancing, Beau and Felicity sat peacefully in front of the fire, sipping coffee.

"My goodness, I'm stiff," she said. "I wonder if I'm up to dancing."

"A few hours of good ol' cowboy jitterbug is just what you need."

Beau's good mood was infectious. "Your Western hospitality has certainly improved since last November, Mr. DuBois."

"Last fall, you were a threat." Beau leaned forward to put his cup on the table and rested his forearms on his knees. "Now I've got you right where I want you."

"Is that so?" Felicity tried to match his bantering tone, but his words challenged her. "And where is that?"

"Bruised and battered and ready to give up."

Felicity stiffened, irritated by his self-assurance. "I'm not about to give up, Beau. If you think one fall from a horse—"

Beau smiled lazily. "Then I'll just have to wear you down on the dance floor."

A reluctant smile tugged at her own lips. "Beau! Be serious."

"Serious?" He raised his brows, feigning surprise. "About dancing?"

As she met Beau's gaze, her laughter died. What was it she read in those dark blue eyes besides the humor? As she watched, his lids dropped lower, and Felicity's heart began to beat faster.

"Felicity—" Beau's voice was rough "—you know what happened last time you looked at me like that. Can I consider this an invitation?"

Felicity licked her lips nervously. "Certainly not. I don't know what you're talking about." She tried to draw a deep breath, but it arrived in her lungs all fluttery. "I wasn't looking any different, Beau."

"Could have fooled me," he murmured almost to himself.

A soft sigh escaped her as he got up to tend the fire. She was overreacting again. She shouldn't let Beau's provocative teasing disturb her so. She and Beau had shared some close moments, but she wasn't naive enough to take his flirting seriously. Even so, as she watched him put another log on the fire, the muscles rippling across his broad back, Felicity felt relieved that she wouldn't be alone with him in Pinedale.

ON THE DRIVE TO PINEDALE, Felicity sat in the front seat of the Cadillac as far from Beau as she could get. When they neared town, Ash pointed out the Wind River mountains that Jacques DuBois had scaled to reach this valley more than a hundred years ago. Their jagged, black shapes looked dangerous and threatening in the moonlight.

Felicity began to feel hemmed in by all the mountains. They looked like a barrier—a vast, distorted wall that might keep her forever in this harsh land. She experienced a rush of homesickness for Florida and her family.

Pinedale was a tiny town at the foot of the mountains with only one paved street. It looked quaintly Western, without the phony facade she'd seen in Jackson. Felicity breathed a sigh of relief at the familiar sight of man-made structures instead of more looming peaks. Smiling to herself, she decided not to tell Beau how charming tourists would probably find this little burg.

As they entered the bar, Felicity glanced around and saw Bobby Jo on a stool, laughing with one of the cowboys. Ash put money in the jukebox and led Cherry onto the tiny dance floor.

Beau pulled Felicity after them. "This will cure your aches and pains," he said.

As her feet began to move in the familiar steps of the jitterbug, Felicity felt her sore muscles limbering up. She had no trouble following Beau's dancing; their bodies seemed perfectly attuned.

When a new song started, Bobby Jo came up to them and cut in. "You don't mind, do you, Felicity?" she said. "This is my favorite song."

Felicity sat down at a table feeling out of place all by herself. The other tables and the dance floor held only couples. Her toe tapped unconsciously to the music, and she caught herself wishing she and Beau had come alone so she wouldn't have to share him with Bobby Jo.

Looking up, Felicity was relieved to see Bud Bonner walking toward her. Glad to have company, she chatted with him eagerly, but her eyes strayed repeatedly to Beau and Bobby Jo.

"I'm sure sorry about what Bobby Jo did to you this afternoon, Felicity," Bud said, interrupting her thoughts. "It's not really you she doesn't like—she just hates the idea of Beau losing his ranch."

Felicity turned angrily to Bud. "Why does everyone blame me? For the hundredth time, I didn't call the Du-Boises—*they* called me. I'm here at Alma's invitation, for heaven's sake."

"I know, I know," Bud said soothingly, holding up a palm to stop the flow of words. "I don't blame you for being riled up. But you can't really blame Bobby Jo, either."

Felicity raised her brows. "I can't?"

Bud shook his head gravely. "Bobby Jo has wanted to live on that ranch as far back as I can remember. Beau's dad and I always sort of figured on those kids marrying. Thing is, they never did fall in love. Beau thinks of Bobby Jo like a sister. And Bobby Jo, well, she's in love with all that land. Our ranch is pretty small, you know, and she's got ranching in her blood."

"She isn't in love with Beau?"

Popping the top on another beer, Bud poured it slowly into his mug. "Well, 'course, she's fond of Beau." He took a healthy swallow. "But I don't think Bobby Jo's ever been in love with a man, just horses and cows. 'Course they've always been good friends, you know. Lots of successful marriages start with less."

The good ones start with a lot more, Felicity thought irritably.

Just then, Beau returned Bobby Jo to the table and took Felicity's hand to lead her back onto the dance floor. She followed willingly, letting her feet respond to the music while her mind went elsewhere. Bobby Jo made her furious. How dare she think of Beau as merely a way to get her hands on a nice big ranch? Beau deserved more than that.

A slow song began, and Beau pulled Felicity into his arms. "Hey, Easterner," he said, slipping his hand down to her waist, "where did you go? I bet you don't even know how many records have played while we danced."

Felicity resisted the gentle pressure of Beau's hand, and held herself stiffly away, not touching his muscular body. "I um, you're right." She lifted her green eyes to his. "My mind was wandering. I'm sorry."

"Thinking about someone you'd rather dance with?" Beau asked.

Felicity shook her head. "To tell the truth, I was thinking about someone you'd rather dance with. Like Bobby Jo."

A broad smile creased Beau's face. "Why would I rather dance with Bobby Jo? If you'd bring your mind back to the dance floor, I wouldn't even mind dancing in public with a dude."

"Very funny."

As Beau steered her around the floor in time to the music, Felicity began to relax in his arms, enjoying his closeness and the musky scent of his after-shave. The pressure of his body moving rhythmically against hers kindled that warm glow inside her—the one she'd vowed to avoid. Leaning her head against his chest, she gave in to the tingling sensations.

"So this is the cowboy jitterbug," she murmured in his ear. "Very nice."

"Mmm..." Beau buried his face in Felicity's flowing auburn hair. "Lucky we have a long cold drive back to the ranch. Maybe I should walk."

Felicity had let her body melt into Beau's, hoping the music would never end, when Bud Bonner, grim-faced, tapped Beau on the shoulder.

"We've got to get home, son," he said. "Big storm's heading in from the north. Bobby Jo and I are leaving now. You'd better get going, too."

A tiny whimper escaped Felicity's lips as Beau gently released her. She couldn't believe a serious storm was coming, not after this beautiful day.

"Go get your coat, Felicity," Beau directed. "These spring storms can move in fast."

Felicity cast him a disbelieving look. "It can't be much of a storm, can it? It's May. It was sixty degrees this afternoon."

Bud smiled without humor. "Well it ain't sixty now—more like thirty and dropping fast." He shrugged. "The only difference between a spring storm and a winter storm is when it's over. Spring snow melts faster."

Felicity's stomach fluttered. "Will we get back to the ranch safely?"

"Sure," said Beau. "If we leave now."

"You'll be fine." Bud looked bleak as he headed for the door. "It's my cows I'm worried about."

A shiver traveled down Felicity's spine. She hadn't even thought about the cattle they'd moved today to summer pasture. If the storm turned out to be a big one, what would happen to all those helpless animals? She stared unseeingly after Bud.

"Felicity—" Beau touched her arm, a teasing grin softening his severe expression "—I know you don't like being ordered around, but all I asked you to do was get your coat."

At Alma's suggestion, Felicity had borrowed a parka from the mudroom. She hadn't needed the big, down-filled coat on the ride to town but now she was glad to have it.

"I was worrying about Bud's cows," Felicity said as Beau helped her into the coat.

"You and me both," he replied, almost as grim-faced as Bud.

When Felicity stepped out of the bar, she was enchanted. Pinedale was transformed. The softly falling snow had covered buildings, sidewalks and trees with a thin layer of white.

"It's like a Christmas card," she exclaimed, turning up her head to catch a falling snowflake on her tongue.

"Come on, Felicity." Beau pulled her toward the car. "The snow's a lot prettier here than it is on the roads. Let's get going before it ices the highway."

Ash and Cherry were waiting in the car. Felicity sat in front, watching Beau's strong hands on the wheel. Her mind filled with questions about the storm and Bud's cows, but when she glanced up at Beau's face and saw his tight jaw, she held her tongue.

"Pretty slick, Beau?" Ash asked.

"Not bad yet," said Beau. "But it won't be long." He glanced at Felicity. "The highways are worse in this weather, Felicity, than in winter. When the road is warm, like today, the snow just melts when it hits, and then the cold air turns it to ice. This could be a nasty drive home."

Felicity couldn't believe they were in any danger. The tiny white flakes falling in the car's headlights looked pretty and harmless; the road just looked wet. Clearly the others disagreed, for a strained silence filled the car.

When they started down a steep hill with several sharp turns, Cherry buried her face in Ash's shoulder. Suddenly the back half of the car began slipping sideways toward the abrupt drop-off. Felicity clutched the dashboard, her scalp prickling at Cherry's terrified gasps.

Beau turned the steering wheel toward the cliff. As the edge came closer and closer, Felicity pushed her fist into her mouth, barely managing to hold back the shriek that rose in her throat. Before Beau regained control of the car, she was sure the tires came within inches of going over.

When he once again had the car pointed in the right direction, Beau exhaled a quiet oath. He took one hand off the wheel long enough to give Felicity's knee a reassuring squeeze. "Pretty exciting, huh?" he said, his gaze fixed on the road. "Better than the big city?"

"That's not funny." Felicity's voice was shaking. "Why did you try to drive us off the cliff?"

Beau chuckled. "Not much black ice in Tampa, is there? If I'd turned away from the skid, we would have gone over the edge. Believe it or not, Felicity, this isn't the first time I've driven on icy roads."

Felicity was still tensely gripping the seat and pushing imaginary brake pedals on the floor. "Thank heavens for that!" she said. "I hope it's not the last, either."

Beau laughed. He seemed completely at ease, not a bit upset by the skid. What a relief to have him at the wheel, Felicity thought. They were down the hill now, and she remembered that the rest of the road, though winding, was relatively flat. Gradually, she willed herself to relax.

Cherry, too, seemed to revive somewhat at the bottom of the hill. "Are you still wondering why I can't live here, Felicity?" she asked in a quavering voice.

"Anyone can learn to drive in the snow, Cherry," Beau said, his eyes flicking back at her in the rearview mirror.

"Not me," Cherry said. She was leaning against Ash, her voice tired and flat. "I tried, remember? I ended up in a ditch."

Ash kissed the top of her head. "That's because you closed your eyes on the curve," he said. "You're lucky you didn't end up around a tree."

"Don't you wonder," Beau mused, giving Felicity a quick glance, "who would go through this twice a day just to go skiing?"

Felicity gazed down the glowing tunnel their headlights cut through the thickly falling snow. "It does seem . . . not quite rational, somehow."

"Hold on to that thought," Beau said.

"No, forget it," Cherry interjected quickly. "Sell the lots in the summer and tell them about the wonderful snow-plows."

A muscle in Beau's jaw twitched slightly, but he didn't respond. Did he think she'd given up on this deal? Felicity wondered. Was that why he wasn't reacting to Cherry's barbs? With a mental shake, Felicity assured herself that one bad storm wasn't enough to change her plans.

At long last they turned into the DuBois ranch road. The ride home had taken almost twice as long as the ride to town. When they got out of the car in the farmyard, Beau turned to Ash.

"I'm going to check on Migs," he said. "She's getting close." He touched the brim of his hat. "G'night, ladies."

Ash draped his arm around Cherry's shoulders and walked slowly toward the house. Felicity started to follow them, but her jangled nerves were still much too keyed-up from the tense drive to let her sleep.

She hurried back to Beau. "Mind if I join you?"

CHAPTER NINE

BEAU LOOKED SURPRISED at Felicity's request. "I'm just going to the barn, Easterner," he said. "Dancing's over for tonight."

Felicity flushed, feeling surprised herself. What on earth made her want to go to a barn, of all places, in the middle of the night, when she could be sleeping contentedly under down and silk?

"I've watched you mend fences, dig postholes, clean irrigation ditches and herd cattle," she said defensively. "Why shouldn't I go with you to check on your horse?"

Beau's features relaxed into a smile. "Why not?"

"Don't you want your coat, Beau?" Cherry called from the porch.

"Yeah," he laughed, "but Felicity's wearing it."

Felicity looked down at the huge parka with sleeves that hung below her hands. No wonder it was so big on her. Beau wore only a natural suede jacket over his black fringed cowboy shirt.

"I can get another, Beau." Felicity started toward the house, but he grabbed her hand.

"You're losing your sense of humor," he said, pulling her with him. "In case you haven't noticed, we natives don't feel the cold as much as you Eastern softies do."

There were several horses in the barn, including Lolo, sleeping in a stall near the door. In another stall at the rear, Migs paced restlessly, throwing her head across her shoulder repeatedly, as though she wanted to see something behind her.

"It's close now," Beau said, his attention focused on Migs. "I'll stay with her just in case she needs me. Horses usually have easy births, but it may be a couple of hours before she really starts. You go on in."

Felicity ignored Beau's dictatorial tone. "I'd rather stay," she said, suddenly sure she'd far rather see this new life come into the world than get a good night's sleep.

"Well..." Beau took Felicity's arms and looked at her dubiously. "Okay, but Migs doesn't know you, and you'll make her nervous. So stay out of her sight. And don't talk."

Felicity wondered if Beau had any idea how bossy he sounded. "Yes, sir."

"Very good," Beau said, smiling. "Give me another week and I'll have you saluting." He entered the mare's stall.

As Felicity watched Beau talking calmly to Migs, stroking her whenever she came close, she felt a strong kinship with the horse. She had never thought much about having children, but now some elemental maternal instinct kindled inside her. *She* wanted to be the one helping Migs.

When Migs lay down for the birth, Beau stood by the side of the stall with Felicity, but his eyes never left the mare.

"Is she all right?" Felicity asked in a whisper.

"Yeah," he replied. "She'll be fine unless—" Beau's gaze was suddenly riveted on the tiny hoof emerging from the mare. "Damn!"

"Beau, what's wrong?" Felicity cried as he rushed to Migs's side.

Beau threw off his jacket and knelt by the horse, quickly rolling up his sleeves. From where she was standing, Felicity couldn't see clearly what he was doing, but he seemed to be trying to force the foal back inside its mother. His face turned red from the strain of his effort, and Migs began to thrash and groan.

"Beau," Felicity pleaded, "what are you doing? You're hurting her!"

Beau's exertion kept him from answering. He was so intent on his task that Felicity wasn't sure he'd heard her.

"Leg caught up," he finally managed to grunt between pushes.

At last, Beau sat back on his heels, rubbing his arm and breathing heavily. The foal's hoof was no longer visible.

"The forelegs should come out together, Felicity," he said, after he'd caught his breath. "Only one came out. The other was stuck inside." He patted the horse's flank. "She'll be all right now."

When Beau stood up, Migs whinnied and kicked, and he went quickly to her head. He made soothing sounds as he sat cross-legged and lifted the horse's head into his lap. Migs soon began to quiet.

"It'll be easier this time, girl," he said, stroking her neck.

When the foal was born, Felicity felt a rush of joy and relief. The tiny new animal lay still on the straw. Pinned beneath Migs's head, Beau looked at it. " Felicity," he cried. "The caul! Get the caul off."

Felicity stared at Beau, wide-eyed. "The what?"

"The membrane over his face." Beau was struggling to get up. "Pull it off! Quick! He's going to suffocate!"

Beau's urgency translated itself to Felicity. She jumped to the colt, grabbed the membrane and ripped it off. The colt's eyes fluttered open and he began to pant. Felicity felt awestruck—had she actually saved this beautiful little creature's life?

Beau pushed a towel into her hand. She immediately dropped to her knees and begun to clean the colt with it.

"No, Dr. Walden," Beau laughed. "The towel's for you. Migs'll take care of her son."

He pulled Felicity to her feet and wiped her hands, then his own with the towel. "Thanks for your help," he said softly, a gleam of admiration in his dark eyes. "You saved his life."

They watched together as Migs cleaned her newborn and urged him to his feet. The tiny, stiff-legged colt raised first one end, then the other. As soon as he was up, he fell, trying to take a step on his unsteady legs. Patiently, Migs helped him up again. This time he managed to take a few cautious steps toward his mother and began to nurse.

Beau rested a foot on the stall railing and gazed at the horses. "This birth was more dramatic than most," he remarked, "but it's always a thrill." He slipped his arm around her shoulders. "Beautiful, huh?"

Feeling tears in her throat, Felicity could only nod. She was surprised Beau could admit such emotions to a woman. The depth of her own feelings surprised her even more. At last she truly understood Beau's conflict: his land and his animals were far more to him than just a piece of real estate.

"We'd better go in," Beau said nudging her away from the stall.

She followed quietly, still too moved to talk. The birth must have awakened Lolo, and Felicity stopped to stroke her.

Beau shoved the barn door shut. "Looks like my prayers have been answered, Felicity." The half smile on his lips belied his serious tone. "You and I are going to spend the night together."

Felicity was shaken out of her soft mood. "Oh no, we're not, Beau DuBois!"

"Just when I thought you'd learned to obey orders." Beau shook his head in mock despair. "Come and see."

He opened the door a crack and flicked off the light so they could see out. A fierce gust blew stinging snow into Felicity's eyes, momentarily blinding her. In her wildest dreams, she couldn't have imagined this much snow. The wind was blowing so hard all the snow seemed to be falling sideways. Every few seconds, large flurries were drawn up and whirled around in huge white eddies.

Fascinated, Felicity opened the door wider and stepped outside. Instantly, she was lost. She was facing into the storm, and icy flakes blew in her eyes, blinding her and forcing her lids shut. Quickly, she spun around, turning her back to the wind, but whirling snow made everything else invisible. The howling wind covered all other sound.

Felicity felt as if she'd fallen into a deep white tunnel. The barn was only a few steps away, but she didn't know which way to go. Fingers of panic clutched at her spine.

Suddenly a square of light cut through the opaque whiteness. Beau had turned the barn light on again. Relief made Felicity weak. As she stumbled toward the lighted door, she saw a huge snowdrift almost as tall as she. How could so much snow have fallen in such a short time?

Beau grabbed her arm and pulled her inside, slamming the door behind them. Shaking violently, Felicity fell against him, panicked by her moments outside the barn and frantic to hold on to another human being.

"I'm the one with no coat on," Beau remarked to no one in particular, "and she's shivering." But he kept his arms wrapped tightly around her until her trembling stopped.

"Beau, that was awful," Felicity said into his shoulder. "I was only outside a minute but I couldn't tell where I was."

"I shouldn't have let you go out," Beau said, stroking her damp hair. "But I figured it was the easiest way to convince you we had to spend the night in the barn."

"It worked like a charm." Felicity shuddered, still gripping Beau's lapels. "Next time, try a little harder to convince me with words, please. I was really scared."

"I'm sorry, Felicity," said Beau. "But sometimes you're very hard to persuade."

"Well, now what?" Felicity pulled away from Beau and looked around the barn, painfully aware of their isolation.

"Where exactly do we sleep?" She glanced down and remembered she was wearing Beau's coat. "Aren't you freezing? How will we ever keep warm?"

Beau's dark eyes glowed as several answers seemed to go through his mind. Finally, with a sigh and a crooked grin, he said simply, "Straw."

He led the way to an empty stall in the middle of the barn, farthest from the doors at either end. He left her there, returning a minute later, carrying several bales of straw and a horse blanket. With a pocketknife, he opened the bales and spread clean straw over the floor of the stall. Felicity lay down, and Beau covered her with the blanket and more straw. She grew slowly warmer beneath rough covers, burrowing a comfortable cocoon into the scratchy straw.

If someone had told her a few weeks ago that getting thrown from a horse, skidding on icy highways and birthing a colt would make her feel more alive than a weekend of tennis and dancing, she'd have laughed. Now, getting caught in a blizzard and sleeping in the barn seemed almost natural. Though she thought longingly of the big water bed in her condo, Felicity knew her desk job would seem pretty tame after these weeks in Wyoming.

Then Beau lifted the blanket and climbed in beside her. Of course, she knew they needed to share their body heat to keep warm. But as he stretched out next to her, Felicity realized that all their clothing, all the straw and all the snow could not curb her response to Beau. She could feel his slightest movement beside her, and she wondered how on earth she would get through the night.

"What if the storm hasn't stopped by morning?" she asked, trying to ignore the feelings Beau's closeness roused in her. "How will we ever get out of here?"

"You little Eastern innocent." A broad smile made Beau's dark eyes twinkle. "Do you think Florida has a monopoly on sunshine? In the daylight we'll be able to see enough to get back to the house even if the storm is still going full force. It isn't very far, you know. We'd probably make it tonight, but we'd be crazy to risk it."

"We sure would." Felicity shuddered, remembering her moments in the blizzard. "But won't everyone be worried about us?"

Beau shook his head. "This won't be the first time I've had to spend the night in the barn." Her heart quickened its beat as he looked at her. "It's just the first time I've enjoyed it."

Felicity lowered her lashes to escape Beau's intense gaze. "You mean this happens all winter?"

"No way," he replied. "We'd freeze to death if we stayed out here in the winter. It's early fall and late spring storms that catch us. In the winter, especially during calving when we're outside every night, we string ropes between the house and the barns." Beau pulled her close. "Do you feel warm enough now, Felicity?"

"Mmm," Felicity murmured, drawing his parka tightly around her. "But I feel guilty about wearing your coat. Isn't there some way we can share it?"

"Not a chance," Beau said. "Too big a risk for an Eastern softie like you. Besides. I'm fine. This jacket is warmer than it looks."

Felicity rolled over and turned her back to Beau. She wished her racing pulse would calm so she could go to sleep, but he curved his body around hers in a way that was disturbing, intimate. Felicity could only assume he was trying to keep warm. After all, she did have his coat on, so she couldn't very well tell him to move away. Besides, she wasn't at all sure she wanted to.

"Beau," she said, fighting the urge to sink back against his body, "I don't think I'm going to get much sleep tonight."

"Me neither," he said, his fingers gently tangling in her silky hair. "Are you worried about your boyfriend? Will he mind that you had to spend the night with me?"

"I don't have a boyfriend." Felicity stiffened, trying to put a little space between them.

"No boyfriend?" Beau urged her closer to fit into the curve of his body. "What's wrong with those men in Florida?"

Felicity pulled free and turned to face him. "The same thing that's wrong with them everywhere," she said firmly. "Fortunately, my career takes most of my time."

Beau reached out to brush a lock of hair from her cheek. "You can't really think *all* men are no good, can you?"

"No, I just..." Embarrassed by Beau's personal questions, Felicity tried to move away, but he grabbed her shoulders and held her facing him.

His fingers gently massaged her upper arms. "You just what?"

"My business is very competitive," Felicity explained, looking down at her hands pressed against his chest. "I'm good at it. That kind of scares men off."

Beau's finger curled under her chin and pushed lightly. "Scared of you, Felicity? All five feet of you?"

"Very funny," she sniffed. "I want more than a physical relationship."

"How very unliberated of you." Beau smiled gently as he stroked a knuckle down her cheek. "Don't tell me you've never met a man who wanted anything more?"

Felicity sighed. "Sometimes it seems that way. Maybe I expect too much." She fluttered a hand through the air. "I guess I've never... heard bells."

"Bells?"

"Oh, you know..." Felicity struggled for the right word. "Been swept away by my feelings for anyone."

"Maybe you won't let yourself feel that way." Beau's understanding tone took the sting out of his words, but Felicity felt a blush staining her cheeks anyway. "Don't you go out at all?"

"Of course I do!" Felicity said. "At least I did before—" Abruptly she clamped her lips shut. This was hardly
the time to start talking about her mother.

For a long moment, Beau simply returned her stare. Then
he took hold of her waist and rolled her over until she had
her back to him. Pulling the coat off her shoulders, he began to massage her tight neck and back muscles. At his first
touch, she stiffened. But the feel of his hands gently knead-
ing away the tension was hard to resist. Soon she felt herself relaxing into his fingers.

"You did before what?" he asked softly, his breath warm
on the back of her neck.

Felicity struggled onto her other side again. A tenderness
she wasn't used to seeing shone from his eyes. She lowered
her lashes. "You don't want to hear all this."

"The hell I don't."

Felicity gazed up at him, unsure. The men she'd dated
wanted fun. Though they sometimes poured out their woes
to her, they expected Felicity to keep her problems to herself. She'd never shared her inner thoughts with a man—
until now.

She took a deep breath. "A year ago my mother had a
stroke. She nearly died." Felicity chewed her lip. "I felt so
guilty."

"You didn't cause her stroke."

"No, but I thought of all the times I'd done something
frivolous instead of visiting Mom." Felicity shuddered despite the warmth she felt from Beau's nearness. "I realized
she was more important to me than the next tennis party. So
I don't date much."

Beau looked angry. "Surely your mother didn't expect
that of you?"

"Oh, no," Felicity said. "Dad kept telling me to go out
more, Mom, too, when she could speak again. But I was so
afraid she'd die while I was out on a date. It was hard to find
a man who didn't begrudge all the time I spent with Mom."

She gave him a shaky smile. "Until we went dancing tonight, I hadn't realized how much I missed it."

"Felicity, that's crazy." Beau cupped her chin in his hand. "You've got your own life to live."

"Do you know how many times I've heard that?"

"Yeah?" His hand slipped to the back of her head and gently massaged her scalp. "Maybe you keep hearing it because it's true."

"I've got my own life." The movements of Beau's fingers made it hard to think. "I've got my job."

"There's more to life than work, Easterner." He traced the line of her jaw with his thumb. "But it sounds like you don't trust men much anyway, do you?"

Felicity fought the warm sensations he was evoking. "I certainly didn't trust *you*, Beau. The day we met was the worst day of my life—the day you threw me out of Wyoming and told me never to come back!"

Beau winced. "I hoped you'd forgotten that."

"Forgotten?" Felicity cried. "How could I forget?"

Beau gave her a lazy smile. "By letting something into your life besides work." His long fingers feathered the hair away from her temples. "Like this." He brushed his lips across her temple toward her ear.

A wave of desire swept over Felicity. Beau must have read it in her face, for he leaned close to kiss her. She desperately wanted to feel his lips on hers, but she turned her head away and pressed her fingertips against his lips. "Beau, if we start kissing now, here—" she waved a hand at their primitive bed "—alone in the barn, you . . . we might not be able to stop."

His hungry eyes met hers. "Damn right."

Felicity couldn't help laughing. At that moment, when her guard was down, Beau's kiss possessed her. As her mouth opened helplessly to the pressure of his, Felicity felt a storm of emotion as turbulent as the one outside, and almost as dangerous. But this time, she wasn't afraid.

She had the strongest feeling this was meant to happen, as though everything that had passed between her and Beau had been building inexorably to this moment. Even Migs and the storm had conspired to throw them together. Felicity couldn't fight the forces of nature. And she couldn't fight the feeling that Beau's lips, so hard yet soft, so gentle yet demanding, were right where they belonged as they moved over hers, deepening the kiss.

Beau's lips made a trail of kisses along her jaw, down her neck to the hollow of her throat, where her pulse throbbed erratically. As his strong hands stroked her waist, he whispered tender endearments in her ear. Then he pulled her against him, and the fire they'd both been ignoring since the moment they met flamed out of control.

Felicity slid her trembling hands inside his soft jacket and pressed them against his heaving chest. Beneath her fingers, his heart pounded like a bass drum.

She hardly noticed when Beau slipped the coat off her shoulders. His hands moved under her blouse, and he groaned softly as he touched her breasts covered by a lacy camisole. Felicity arched her neck and threw back her head, drowning in the sweet sensations.

Deep inside, she felt a liquid warmth, as though all her bones were dissolving. But it was more than simple desire she felt. Beau had awakened a part of her she'd never known, recognized a need in her no other man had ever seen.

Beau kissed her again and again, deep demanding kisses that took her higher and higher, toward a peak she somehow sensed she could share only with him. Felicity kissed him back, awed by the rich masculine taste of him. She felt, rather than heard, his hoarse voice moaning her name.

Beau caught her face between his palms and showered it with kisses. "I want you, Felicity," he murmured huskily. "I need you. If you're not ready for this, you'd better stop me now, or you won't be able to stop me at all."

Felicity didn't understand. Her rational mind had long since ceased to function. She could think now only with her heart, and her heart said yes.

Focusing her gaze on Beau, she saw that his eyes were inky with desire. Her shaking fingers outlined his full lips as she responded in a breathy whisper, hardly knowing what she was saying, "Not ready? How can you ask me that?"

"You know what I mean," he answered in a voice thick with passion.

Felicity shook her head, completely unaware of the trusting, vulnerable look in her eyes. "Beau, I've never..."

Pulling her hard against his chest, Beau swore softly but expressively under his breath. She could feel his heart pounding as he buried his face in her tousled hair. "No, Felicity." He shuddered. "This just isn't right."

Felicity felt as if he'd struck her. She flushed hot with shame. She had willingly offered herself to Beau, and he'd turned her down. She struggled furiously to be free of his strong arms, but he held her tight, calming her.

Felicity lifted her head and looked into Beau's blue eyes, now almost black with desire. Mirrored there, she saw all that she was feeling.

"Why did you stop?" she finally asked, hoping her voice didn't tremble. "Did I do something wrong?"

A spasm crossed Beau's face. "Oh, no," he said hoarsely. "You did everything exactly right. But it wouldn't be fair to you, Felicity." He cradled the back of her head in his palm. "This is your first time, isn't it?"

Felicity was too shaken at the moment to tell him it was none of his business. "I...never felt this...I mean..."

"Ah, Easterner," Beau said huskily. "I can't take advantage of your innocence and a freak snowstorm to seduce you in a barn on a dirty old horse blanket." He carefully tucked a wispy curl behind her ear and brushed his lips across her temple. "Not your first time. You deserve better."

"Better?" she asked, tracing his lips with her still trembling fingers. "How could it be better?"

"Felicity, don't push me," Beau groaned. "I want you. I'm a man, not a saint. How much do you think I can take?"

She ran the back of her hand across his whiskered jaw. "I think..." She hesitated. "I'm trying to find out."

Beau stilled her caressing fingers with a grip so tight it hurt. "Don't try to find out, Felicity." An edge of seriousness sharpened his deep voice. "Until you know you can handle it."

Felicity picked some straw out of his hair. She ached to make love to him. But his tender concern touched her deeply. She looked up at him and caressed his cheek. He returned her gaze, his eyes still full of desire. Felicity longed to lose herself in the flame that still smoldered between them.

But maybe Beau was right—maybe this wasn't the right time or the right place. And maybe this wasn't the right man. She had waited twenty-three years. Shouldn't she keep waiting until she was absolutely sure? Her feelings for Beau had grown immeasurably the past few weeks, but what did she really feel? Was it only the pull of his overwhelming masculinity? Or was there something more?

"Felicity, stop!" Beau begged in an agonized tone, his fingers biting into her shoulders.

With a start, Felicity realized her hand had left Beau's cheek to gently massage his chest. Her green eyes met his dark blue ones, and the intensity of emotion she saw there shocked her. Beau was just barely restraining himself. How much longer could he hold out, with her wrapped in his arms this way?

"Beau," she asked, her voice still quivering slightly, "how will we sleep?"

"Not like this!"

Felicity flinched with hurt, though she knew his gruffness was not directed at her. He rolled away and stood up.

"You sleep," he ordered, "I'll pace. It'll keep me warm enough."

"No, Beau, I'll..." Felicity started to get up, too, but Beau's big callused hands pressed her roughly back onto the straw and held her there.

"Just this once, you liberated little Easterner," he growled, "will you do what you're told?"

Felicity realized she had pushed him too far; a glint in his eyes warned her not to test him any further. "If you're not going to stay under this blanket," she said meekly, "will you at least wear your coat? You'll freeze, Beau."

"If I get cold, I'll just look at you and let my imagination run wild." He sighed. "I don't need the coat, Felicity, and you do. Now put it on and go to sleep. Please."

"Fat chance," she sniffed, wriggling into the coat. Not for a minute did she think she could sleep. Not with Beau pacing nearby, watching her.

Without his warmth under the blanket, Felicity felt cold seeping in. She pulled the coat tightly around her, more worried than ever about Beau in his thin jacket. The dizzying excitment she had felt in Beau's arms gradually subsided, but what would happen tomorrow if the storm still raged, and they were trapped here all day, the two of them alone in the barn?

CHAPTER TEN

WHEN FELICITY AWOKE, yawning and stretching, she felt something warm and hard pressed against her body. Her eyes popped open to find Beau lying next to her, his unshaven face propped on one hand, eyes gazing into hers. Quickly she squirmed away, putting a few inches between them in their makeshift bed. As she looked into his sleepy blue eyes, memories of last night's lovemaking flooded her senses. Flushing, Felicity lowered her lashes.

"Rise and shine, sleepyhead," Beau said.

Felicity combed her fingers through her tangled hair. "Are you the reason I felt so warm all night?"

"Of course." He brushed a wispy curl off her cheek, smiling tiredly. "I got back under the blanket as soon as you fell asleep."

"Thank heavens," Felicity said, relieved he hadn't spent the whole night pacing in the cold. "Did you get any sleep?"

"Not a wink." He rubbed a fist across his bristly chin. "But at least I was warm."

Felicity shivered as a gust of wind howled outside the barn. "I suppose the snow has stopped and it's a beautiful spring day?" she said without much conviction.

Beau's half smile deepened the corners of his mouth. "I doubt it. But it's five o'clock and I'm confident the sun has come up, just as I predicted. Let's go look."

Felicity pulled the blanket tight around her and snuggled into the straw. Her tingling nerves reminded her how small a space separated her body from Beau's. She felt so warm and protected here with him that she hated to get up. Just the thought of leaving the safety of their bed to venture out into that blizzard made her shudder.

"Why don't we wait awhile," she suggested, pulling a few strands of straw from Beau's dark curls, "and see if the snow stops?"

Beau raised his brows. "How long would you suggest? Two or three days?"

"That sounds perfect," Felicity murmured, nestling against him in the straw.

"Oh no, you don't." Beau took Felicity's hand and hauled her to her feet. "Up and at 'em, woman."

He brushed the straw off her back and legs, then they went to check on Migs. As she watched the colt nurse, Felicity felt a rush of pride, remembering her part in his birth.

She could have watched the horses all day, but Beau turned her toward the door. When he opened it, Felicity almost cried. The only thing illuminated by the daylight was more snow—so much that Felicity could see nothing else. But as she continued to peer into the white swirling clouds, she dimly saw the outline of the house a few hundred yards away.

"I guess if we can see it we can get there, right?" she asked, gripping the sleeve of Beau's jacket.

"Right." Beau smiled down at her. "No sweat. Just keep thinking about breakfast and a roaring fire, and follow me."

"Follow you?" Felicity's voice tightened in alarm. "Can't I hold on to you?"

"Of course." Beau gave her shoulders a reassuring squeeze. "I mean stay behind me. I'll block the wind and it'll be easier for you to walk."

He reached for Felicity's hand. At his touch, her pulse fluttered and began to race. She took a long slow breath, wishing they were still under the blanket.

"Beau," she said, tightening her fingers around his, "I—"

Beau's jaw muscles tensed. "Let's go," he said gruffly, "I've got work to do."

He pulled her out the door and into the fury of the storm. Felicity immediately moved into the shelter of his broad back. Even following so closely, she could barely see him in front of her. When she tried to look around him, blustering wind hurled snow into her eyes and forced them shut. She wondered how Beau managed to see at all. Several times Felicity staggered and almost fell in the deep drifts. She yelled at Beau to go a little slower, but her voice was drowned out by the shriek of the wind.

After what seemed like miles, they stumbled up the back steps and into the mudroom. Beau leaned against the wall, breathing hard. He was soaked to the skin in his light jacket, and Felicity could see dark curls pressing against his wet shirt as his chest heaved. Her large coat—Beau's coat—and his broad body had protected her, but her hair was dripping and her face stung from the biting snow.

"Felicity," Beau said, as he regained his breath, "next time Mom tells you to borrow her blue parka, she means this one." He held up a much smaller coat the same color as the one she was wearing.

"Oh, fiddle." Felicity gave him a sheepish grin. "If you'd had a coat, you might have paced all night."

"True," he said, holding up his palms in defeat. "How about a hot bath?"

"Sounds like heaven."

Later, when she reluctantly emerged from the steaming bath, Felicity found, carefully laid out on her bed, a set of pretty, lace-trimmed long underwear. She flushed as she fingered the soft wool. Only Beau would have slipped into her room to leave this intimate gift. But he must have been right outside her door while she was naked in the tub.

As she dried and brushed her long thick hair, she wondered what she would have done if Beau hadn't merely left his gift and slipped away. What if he'd been waiting when she finished her bath? Tingling at the thought, Felicity realized that even now, with her mind unclouded by passion, she was still confused about Beau.

She'd felt very close to him the last few days, especially after their talk in the hot tub and...last night. He could make her madder than anyone she'd ever met—or gladder—or sadder. In fact, all her feelings seemed more intense around Beau. It made her wonder if she'd actually, for the first time in her life, fallen in love.

Oh, come *on*, Felicity, she chided herself. Get out of the clouds. She returned her attention to the blow dryer.

When Felicity entered the kitchen in search of coffee, Beau was standing at the stove watching three sizzling pans. "I was afraid you'd drowned," he said, glancing up. "Coffee's ready."

In the still sleeping house, the kitchen was a haven of quiet warmth, isolated from the rest of the world by the falling snow outside. Felicity sipped her coffee and watched Beau's movements as he cooked, his dark hair curling over his collar, his jeans low on his hips. Could he feel her presence as strongly as she felt his?

"Are you too close to the stove, Felicity?" Beau asked, handing her a filled plate. "Your face is flushed."

Felicity dropped her eyes. "No," she murmured. "It's nice here."

Beau sat down across the table from her. "You're right," he said, touching her under the chin. "It's nicer than usual. Now this morning, Easterner, you eat."

As the tantalizing aromas from their plates wafted up to her, Felicity realized she was famished. She devoured bacon, eggs, hash browns and hotcakes. Finally, she sat back replete and looked up at Beau, who had eaten twice as much.

"A man who can cook," she said. "Will you never stop surprising me, Beau DuBois?"

A smile tilted Beau's lips. "Not if I can help it."

Ash came through the door in his stocking feet. "I really thought we were through with long johns this year," he grumbled, as he took a plate to the stove.

He was wearing wool-lined jeans with a turtleneck under his heavy wool shirt. Felicity noticed for the first time that Beau was dressed the same way. With a sudden shock, she realized they planned to go outside in this ghastly weather.

"Most of the hands are here," said Ash, spreading butter on his hotcake. "Chick called 'em all and got the bunkhouse ready as soon as he heard about the storm."

"Good." Beau tipped back his chair to reach the coffee pot and refilled their mugs. "We'll need 'em."

Ash cast a curious glance at Felicity. "Did you have to sleep in the barn?"

"Yep." Beau's voice sounded casual but his dark eyes flashed a warning at his brother. "Migs foaled. Beautiful little stud colt."

Felicity's cheeks felt warm again. Thank goodness Beau had turned the conversation away from their night in the barn.

"Chick said he'd have the teams ready by seven," Ash said, avoiding Felicity's eyes, "so we can feed from the sleds."

"You can't mean you're going out in that awful storm, just as though it's a normal day?" Shocked, Felicity stared out the window at the white wall of snow.

Beau's eyes were serious as he answered. "The cows have to be fed, Felicity. Cows have more trouble in this kind of weather than most animals."

"Why?" She couldn't imagine an animal that wouldn't have trouble in this weather.

"They can't kick away the snow," Beau said with a shrug. "This time of year, there's grass right under their feet, but they can't get at it."

Felicity poured more coffee, hoping the men would take the time to drink it. "Are they very far away?"

"No, they're still in winter pasture, where they're easy to feed." Beau ran a hand through his unruly curls. "That's why we move them down in the winter."

"How can anything survive in a storm like this?" Felicity asked. "What about those antelope we saw yesterday?"

Beau snorted. "They're probably out in my field right now, munching away on last year's haystack."

"They aren't if Chick's spotted 'em," Ash stated bluntly.

"How can you sound so mean about such beautiful animals?" Felicity said. "I'd let them eat all they wanted."

Beau shook his head at her naiveté. "You wouldn't if it meant your herd would starve," he said. "This late in the spring, it doesn't matter much, but we don't want them to get used to it. If it were winter, we'd have to do something about them."

Felicity looked at him curiosuly. "Like what?"

Beau softly touched her cheek. "We'd shoot them, Felicity."

Felicity's jaw dropped as she stared at Beau. How could he look so kind, while he was saying something so cruel? But his compassion was for her, she realized, because he knew she was upset by his words, not for the antelope. So hard and so soft—which was the real Beau?

Felicity sipped her coffee and watched snow blowing against the window, while Ash and Beau went into the mudroom to dig out their winter gear. She heard considerable good-natured arguing over boots and chaps, when suddenly silence fell.

Felicity went to the mudroom door to see what had happened. Ash and Beau looked like two big clumsy bears in all their winter clothes. Besides mittens, a stocking hat with a mask and long leather chaps, Beau was wearing a red-and-black-checked wool coat. Ash stood staring at his brother, his own parka dangling from his hand.

"Beau?" Ash said, sounding dazed. "What . . ."

Beau gave him a friendly punch on the arm. "Better step on it. You know how Chick grumbles when we're late."

Ash opened his mouth to respond, then closed it again.

Beau pulled his cap down and opened the door. "See you at lunch, Felicity."

Ash stared at the door Beau had closed behind him. "That was Dad's coat," he mumbled.

Felicity turned to him. "Won't it keep Beau warm?"

"Yeah, sure. It's just…" Ash poked his arms into his own coat and zipped it up. His bewildered eyes met Felicity's. "After Dad died, I wanted to give his coat to Bud, but Beau wouldn't let me. He was furious. He insisted he'd wear it himself, but he never did." Ash's gaze returned to the closed door. "Until today."

"Until today," Felicity repeated, feeling a little awed by Ash's words. She, too, turned to stare at the place where Beau had stood, and a warm glow started deep inside her.

"How long will you be, Ash?" she asked as he pulled open the door. "I mean if you're not back by a certain time, should I do something?"

"What would you do?" Ash sounded interested.

A hint of a smile touched Felicity's lips. "Call the weather bureau and complain?"

"That'd help a lot." Ash laughed. "Try it. We'll be back in a few hours."

As the door shut behind him, Felicity looked at her watch and felt a rush of sympathy for Cherry. No wonder she hated it here in the winter. A few weeks of this and a wife would be a psychiatric case.

Felicity cleaned up the kitchen, trying without success to take her mind off Beau out in the storm. She couldn't help remembering his concern last night for Migs and her colt; he'd have spent all night with the horse's head in his lap if she'd needed him. Now he was risking his life to feed his cows.

Felicity put down the dish towel. She'd have to be a fool not to realize that Beau would never agree to turn this ranch into a resort. But if he'd just listen to her idea about the lake, surely he'd see it was the answer for everyone in the family. Especially him.

Felicity looked out the kitchen window, but she couldn't see anything through the frozen patterns on the glass except swirling white. If anything, the storm had worsened since she and Beau had come in from the barn.

Frustrated, Felicity grabbed Alma's coat and went out the back door. In the shelter of the porch, Felicity could keep her eyes open despite the wind. She peered fruitlessly into the white murkiness of the blizzard. A drift came up almost to the kitchen window; another completely covered the windward side of the porch. Felicity couldn't even glimpse the big red barns.

Slowly, a looming shape appeared, almost obscured by snow. It was a huge flat sled piled high with hay bales, pulled by a team of the big Belgian horses she'd seen Chick grooming yesterday. Felicity knew one of the three men on the sled was Beau, though she could barely see his form through the churning blizzard.

When he saw her, Beau waved and jumped off the sled. He ran up to Felicity and pushed back his wool mask.

"What the devil are you doing out here?" he asked impatiently. "Get inside."

"I couldn't see anything out the window," Felicity told him. "It was frustrating."

"There's nothing to see in this weather except snow." Beau sounded exasperated. "You can see that just fine out the window."

"Where's Ash?" Felicity asked, trying to deflect Beau's irritation while prolonging their conversation.

"He's on another sled." Beau's mittened hand clasped Felicity's arm and propelled her firmly toward the door.

"We're using all three sleds, so we won't be long. It's a big help having the hands here."

Resisting his pressure, Felicity turned to him again. "Are you sure you'll be all right?"

A look of understanding softened Beau's face. "Felicity, believe me, I've done this a million times. I'm only going a few hundred yards. Now get inside, and keep the fire going for me. I'll be back before you know it."

He gave her a final shove toward the door, ran back to the sled and swung easily onto the bales. The big workhorses had never stopped plodding.

Felicity went into the dining room and glared at the fire. How did women live here? she wondered, jabbing at the coals. Tending fires couldn't hold their attention long. Even in this awful weather, Felicity would rather have been out helping Beau, than sitting there worrying about whether he was alive or dead.

She moved restlessly toward the kitchen. Alma was standing next to the sink chopping vegetables.

"Where's Cherry?" Felicity asked.

"Cherry always sleeps as late as she can during bad weather," Alma explained. "She hopes Ash'll be home by the time she gets up."

Felicity and Alma had finished preparing homemade vegetable soup and Reuben sandwiches, when Cherry finally appeared. She was dressed in faded jeans and a rumpled gray flannel shirt that must have belonged to Ash. Her blond hair hung limply around her pale face.

Felicity was shocked. Where was the sophisticated New York model she'd come to know? Cherry wandered aimlessly around the kitchen, sipping her coffee and peering out the window every few minutes. Felicity, who had almost convinced herself Beau was in no danger, felt her own anxiety increase dramatically as she watched Cherry.

"You see what this does to me?" Cherry quavered, waving her hands. "And this goes on all winter. Of course,

sometimes the snow stops. But when it's forty below outside, it's just as bad. Do you know how fast you can freeze
to death at forty below?''

"Cherry—" Alma began just as Beau and Ash came
padding into the kitchen in their stocking feet.

Relief surged through Felicity, and Cherry rushed into
Ash's arms. Felicity had to grip the salt shaker till her fingers hurt to keep from following Cherry's example and
throwing herself at Beau.

Watching Beau's tired face as he wolfed down his food,
Felicity ached to touch him. She wanted to brush the damp
curls from his brow, kiss the sparkle back into his heavy-
lidded eyes. She took a mouthful of her soup, but it landed
in her stomach like a pound of lead. Felicity wondered what
was wrong with her. Of course, she was glad Beau had returned unhurt, but surely this possessive light-headed feeling was an overreaction!

Cherry hovered around Ash while he ate, rubbing his
shoulders and stroking his cheek. Unlike Beau, he seemed
to revive completely with lunch. But both men were still very
restless. Felicity was confused—weren't their chores done
for the day?

"Did you feed my chicken, boys?" Alma asked.

"Yes, Mom," Beau rubbed his eyes, for once not re-
sponding to his mother's good humor.

"Beau," Felicity finally said, "you need some rest. Why
aren't you on your way to bed?" Color rushed to her cheeks
as she recalled why Beau was so tired.

"You still don't get it, do you, Felicity?" Cherry's lips
twisted into a bitter grin. "You think they're all done for the
day, don't you? Ha, ha. Not them. Not the wonder boys of
Hoback Valley."

"Stop it, Cherry," Beau said grimly.

Felicity looked into Beau's weary eyes, wondering what
Cherry meant. Beau steadily returned her gaze. Suddenly

Felicity knew what no one was telling her, and her heart stopped.

"You're going to feed Bud's cows." Fear made her voice unnaturally high.

"Of course we are," said Beau.

"You can't mean it!" Felicity tried not to shriek. "You're going all the way up on that ridge in this storm? That's insane!"

"Of course, it's insane." Cherry twisted her fingers through Ash's. "Don't think that's going to stop them."

"It's our job, Felicity. We're just doing what we have to do." Beau lifted his shoulders in a shrug. "There are a couple of hundred animals and several humans depending on us. Bud is desperate. That's most of his life up there."

"But how will you get there?" Felicity shuddered, thinking of that steep, winding road they'd taken the cows up yesterday. "Your horses must be tired already—they won't make it up that hill in this weather. You'll never get back before dark."

"Less than a month in Wyoming," Beau said, a crooked grin flitting over his mouth. "and you're going to tell me how to ranch?"

"We'll tow the sled up with the Cat, Felicity," Ash told her. "Mike Weber will go with us. He drives the snowplow for the county."

"What's a Cat?" Felicity asked.

"It's a bulldozer," Beau said patiently. "It'll move the snow—well, some of it—but it isn't too big to get up the road. We use it to plow snow around here in the winter."

"How will we know..." Felicity chewed her lip. "Do you have a radio?"

Beau shook his head. "A CB probably couldn't reach that far anyway, but in this storm, it'd be useless." He drained his coffee and pushed back his chair. "I told Bud we'd leave about noon," he said to Ash, avoiding Felicity's eyes, "so we can't sit around here too long. Chick and the boys'll have the sled loaded pretty soon."

"Is there much risk, Beau? Truly?" Felicity asked. She was beginning to find Cherry's near-hysteria understandable.

"The only risk is getting stuck in a snowdrift," Beau said, the weariness showing in his tone. "If we were too far from the road, we might freeze to death before we got help, but it's unlikely. We'll be dressed for the weather and it isn't very cold. We can walk several miles when it's like this."

"If it doesn't get any colder," said Cherry bitterly. "And if you don't get wet or hurt. And if you don't get stuck too far from help. And if you don't use all your strength trying to dig out. And if—"

"All right, Cherry, all right." Ash stood and took his wife by the shoulders. "There's some risk, but we'll be much safer than you imagine. Try not to worry, okay?" Giving her a quick kiss, he gently pushed her into a chair and glanced at Alma. "Take care of her, Mom?" With a worried look at Cherry, he turned to Beau. "Let's go."

Felicity felt her throat constrict as she watched Beau leave the kitchen. She wanted to say goodbye but she couldn't speak. She was afraid her voice would show too much emotion.

When she heard the back door slam, Felicity left the kitchen and wandered aimlessly through the house. In the office where she'd phoned Scotty, she sank into the desk chair and rested her head on her arms, trying to calm her frantic nerves. If she hadn't lived through the near-death of her mother such a short time ago, she might not be so afraid for Beau now. But this waiting helplessly for news of a loved one—

A loved one? Startled by the thought, Felicity lifted her head, eyes wide. Did she mean that? She couldn't deny that she enjoyed being with Beau more than she thought was wise, or that his kisses moved her in a way no man's ever had. But did that mean she loved him?

Suddenly the phone caught Felicity's eyes. On impulse, she lifted the receiver and dialed her parents' number. Her mother's voice sounded clear and close, but Felicity couldn't help thinking about how far away she was.

"Hi, Mom," she said, annoyed at the tremor in her voice.

"Felicity?" Her mother seemed surprised. "What's wrong?"

Felicity forced her voice to sound normal. "How's the weather down there?"

"It's lovely," Clarissa said cheerfully. "But don't tell me you called to ask about the weather."

"It's snowing here," Felicity said. "In May. Isn't that crazy?"

"Crazy." Felicity could almost hear her mother shaking her head. "Is that what's upsetting you so, dear? Snow? Or are you going to tell me what you really called about?"

"Oh, Mom." Felicity took a deep breath. "Beau...I mean, Mr. DuBois...I mean, the man I'm doing business with here...he's out in the storm now. And I'm so afraid for him."

"Surely a storm, even a big storm, must be all in a day's work for him."

"Not this time," Felicity said. "He's going much farther than he usually does in the winter. It's kind of complicated, but take my word for it, he's risking his life."

"Did he tell you that?" Clarissa asked.

"Well, no," Felicity admitted. "He said there wasn't much risk."

"Then why are you so worried, dear? He's a rancher. He must know what he's doing." After a pause, Clarissa added, "What's this Beau like?"

"Oh, he's..." Felicity's voice trailed off. How could she possibly describe Beau in a few words? "Well, he's got dark eyes and curly hair and...rough hands but a soft heart."

Clarissa laughed. "He sounds charming. And I take it—" Felicity could imagine the knowing look in her mother's eyes "—you've been charmed?"

"Mom, I'm so mixed up." Felicity twisted a curl around her finger. "I've only known him a few weeks. I don't know what I feel."

"Well, I can't answer that for you, dear," said Clarissa. "Only your heart can tell you that."

"I know. You're right." Felicity sighed. "How are you?"

"I'm fine. Your father and I are just leaving to play bridge at the club."

"You're kidding," Felicity said. "Dad hates bridge."

"Yes, and you know how I feel about golf, but this morning I caddied for him."

"Caddied?" Felicity exclaimed. "Mom, you can't do things like caddy! You're not—"

"Now don't start fussing," Clarissa said, and Felicity could hear the laughter in her voice. "I just drove the golf cart."

"Oh." Felicity felt somewhat mollified. "I guess you two just want to do things together, huh?"

"We know better than most couples how precious our time together is." Clarissa's voice softened. "I don't love golf, but I do love Matt. And Felicity, you remember what *we* did when we'd known each other three weeks."

"What?"

"We got married." Clarissa's quick laugh sounded over the wire. "I've got to run, dear. Bye."

Felicity smiled at the phone, wishing she knew her heart as well as her mother had thirty-three years ago. A sudden gust of wind made snow clatter against the window, bringing her mind back to Beau in the storm. Not wanting to be alone any longer, she left the chilly office and hurried back to the kitchen.

Cherry sat at the table with her head in her arms. The room seemed empty without the men.

Felicity gazed out the window. "Do you thing they've gone?"

"Probably not," Alma said from the sink where she was doing the dishes. "They had to help Chick load the sled."

Felicity felt abandoned. The emptiness she'd felt when Beau left this morning was multiplied a thousandfold now. She stared at Alma, her shoulders sagging.

Cherry raised her head and spoke in a wail. "I thought it was over for this year. I can't stand it again. He's never coming back."

Alma turned to her. "Of course, he'll be back, Cherry."

"Not this time," Cherry cried. "I know it. No one's ever tried to get to the ridge in a storm. The pasture's too far away, the road's too steep and narrow. They'll never make it." She dropped her head back on her arms and her quavery words were muffled. "I'll never see him again, never again, never...."

Alma gave Felicity an alarmed glance as she hurried to Cherry's side and put both arms around her shoulders. "They'll make it, Cherry. They do this all winter, you know that. Don't be scared."

Cherry's voice rose to a howl. "I want Ash. Please let me see Ash." Sobbing uncontrollably, she clutched at Alma. "Don't let him go this time. Please."

Panic rose in Felicity's throat. How could they ever find Ash in the blizzard? Cherry's sobs grew louder and more hysterical as she begged Alma to bring Ash back to her.

Something had to be done. Felicity touched Alma on the shoulder and spoke quietly. "I'll go find Ash."

"No, no, Felicity." Alma's voice tightened anxiously. "Cherry, why don't you take one of those sleeping pills Doc prescribed for you? You'll feel much better."

"No!" Cherry shrieked. "If I go to sleep, Ash will be dead when I wake up. I know it, I just know it."

Alma looked over Cherry's head at Felicity. "I'd better go look for him."

"No, Alma, don't leave me." Cherry tightened frantic arms around her mother-in-law. "Don't go. Stay with me. Just get Ash here. He'll die. Don't leave me," she gasped between racking sobs.

"You can't leave her like this," Felicity said. "I'll have to go. Won't they come by the porch like they did this morning? I can catch them."

"Maybe you'd better," Alma said helplessly, as Cherry continued to wail. "She's never been this bad before. But don't step off the porch until you see them." She looked fiercely at Felicity. "Promise me you won't step off that porch until you see them. And no matter what, don't lose sight of the house."

Felicity remembered the way she'd felt last night in the blizzard and how helpless she'd felt this morning even in the shelter of Beau's body. "Don't worry," she said. "I promise."

Actually she was relieved to be doing something. Anything seemed better then sitting around worrying about Beau. She grabbed Alma's blue coat and found a scarf, stocking hat and mittens. With the warm woolen underwear Beau had left for her, she felt completely protected. Knotting the scarf around her neck, she stepped out into the cold.

Felicity stood on the back porch, trying to get her bearings. The barns and sheds were completely invisible now, and the howling wind covered all other noise. She huddled in the shelter of the snowdrift, her eyes straining into the storm. Time seemed to stop, and Felicity had no idea how long she'd been outside when she saw, off on the right, a large shadowy shape that must be the hay sled. It had come from that direction this morning. Thank heavens, she thought, remembering Cherry's shrieks.

"Beau!" shouted Felicity, waving excitedly.

The sound of her voice was swallowed by the storm. They were so close, she couldn't let them get away. Surely, she could catch them. Steeling herself, Felicity struck off toward the shape.

As soon as she left the shelter of the porch, her helpless feeling of last night returned, but she kept on. The sled could only be a few steps away. It wasn't dark now, but in this raging maelstrom it might as well have been. The wind pushed Felicity in this direction and that, leaving her breathless. The sharp stinging snow hit her face with enough force to hurt. Most of the time she couldn't get her eyes open, so she just kept walking in the same direction.

Her cheeks started to sting cruelly. No wonder Beau wore a wool mask in this weather. She tried to wrap her scarf around her face, but the wind snatched it from her hand and blew it away. Felicity turned, desperately grabbing at the scarf, only to see it rapidly disappear in the wailing white turbulence.

The brightly colored scarf had been visible for only a few seconds. With a shock, Felicity realized she couldn't possibly have seen the hay sled a hundred yards away. Then what on earth was she heading for?

Terror gripped her. She had no idea how far she'd walked. Frantically she turned around and around, looking for the house. Blowing snow made everything invisible. But she had to try to get back to the house, whether she could see it or not. If only this vicious wind would stop for just a moment so she could really get her eyes open.

Felicity had turned around so much she didn't know in which direction she'd been walking. Hadn't she been facing into the wind? At least some of the time? But when she'd stood on the back porch, the wind hadn't been blowing right at her—hadn't it been blowing across the porch? Which way? She couldn't remember. She had no idea which way to go.

Felicity wanted to fall down and sob, but she forced herself to start walking. She'd walked across this yard with Beau dozens of times in the past few weeks. Surely something familiar would show up. If she kept moving, at least she had a chance of finding shelter, perhaps even the house. Every few seconds she called for Beau, though she could hardly hear herself over the shriek of the wind.

Felicity had no idea how long she walked and stumbled in the storm. Most of the time, she kept her eyes closed. Every time she tried to look around, the wind lashed her eyes with biting snow, making them smart and close involuntarily. After a time, she stopped trying to see. It was too depressing to keep looking for help and see only white nothingness.

For all Felicity knew, she might have been walking in circles. Snow and wind, wind and snow filled her world. She got colder and tireder with every step until all her muscles ached. At least her cheeks had stopped their painful throbbing.

When she was sure she couldn't take another step, Felicity stumbled against a building. At first she thought it was merely another big snowdrift; she'd begun to think that all the world was made of snow. But as her hands felt the solidness of a wall, relief coursed through her. Clumsily, she groped around the building until she found the door, opened it and fell inside.

Finally out of the howling storm, Felicity lay collapsed on the floor, panting with relief at her good fortune. At last she forced herself to stand up and close the door. And then she felt another stab of fear. She hadn't found a barn with straw bales and warm animals, where she could probably live for days. She'd stumbled into some sort of equipment shed, filled with tractors and trucks. Snow still clung to her hat and mittens, and it wasn't melting. Whatever had made her think long underwear was going to keep her warm in this ghastly weather?

Shivering, Felicity took stock of her situation. With Cherry weeping and clinging to her, Alma might not notice Felicity had left the porch until it was too late to catch Beau and Ash before they started for the ridge. Chances were, no one was looking for her. She would have to get back to the house on her own.

Clamping her chattering teeth, Felicity opened the door, took one look outside and slammed it shut. She would stay here. Someone would look for her, sooner or later. No matter how long it took, she'd wait. Nothing could make her go back out in that storm alone.

Besides, she thought looking around hopefully, this might be where they kept the bulldozer. If so, Beau would find her when he returned. Surely she could keep herself warm for a few hours. Beating her arms across her chest, Felicity tried to find a sheltered corner of the shed, but the heavy metal equipment seemed to exude cold.

Well, in here at least she had a chance; outside she'd had none. Felicity tensed her muscles tighter and tighter to stop her shivering. She just couldn't freeze to death now. Not without seeing Beau again, not without finding the answer in her heart.

When I make a stupid mistake, she thought, leaning against the wall of the shed, *it's a doozy.*

Well, she wouldn't give up; she'd have to believe Beau would find her when he returned. *If* he returned. Life couldn't be that cruel, could it? To snatch Beau away from her just as she thought she was falling in love with him? Before she knew if he loved her?

Desperate to keep warm, Felicity fought the sleepiness stealing over her. She knew she had to stay awake, knew the worst thing she could do was fall asleep. She tried pacing from one cold wall to another, counting her steps. Her knees felt like ice water and all her limbs were so heavy, it was hard to keep moving.

Thirteen, fourteen, was Cherry all right? Fifty-eight, fifty-nine, surely Beau would come soon. Eighty-one, eighty-t...keep moving...eighty... Maybe she would rest for just

a minute. *Won't sleep,* she promised herself as she crumpled to the concrete floor, *just close my eyes for a second.*

"Stay awake," she mumbled aloud. "Wait for Beau ...
few hours ... not long."

For the first time since she'd left the house, Felicity felt
warmth flowing in her veins. Or was it numbness? She
couldn't tell, and she didn't care. Oblivion seemed so much
more pleasant than waiting for help that might never come.

Love you, Beau, Felicity's heart told her, as her eyelids
fluttered shut.

CHAPTER ELEVEN

FOR THE SECOND TIME that day, Felicity opened her eyes to see Beau gazing down at her. His eyes moved anxiously over her face, his features drawn with fear. Behind him stood Chick Hollings.

Felicity blinked slowly, trying to think. Beau was back—or hadn't he gone? It didn't matter; he was here with her now. She looked into his handsome, worried face and tried to say, "I love you," but her lips moved thickly, without sound.

"Felicity, Felicity." Beau shook her by the shoulders. "Are you all right? Talk to me."

"Um...fine," she mumbled. Her words were barely audible, slurred and groggy. "Be fine...once you quit... shaking me."

"Oh, no!" Beau's voice sounded strangled. "Listen to her. She has hypothermia!"

Felicity didn't notice the cold now, though she felt very lazy and heavy-limbed; her mind wouldn't work right. Beau sounded so upset, and she couldn't understand why. She was safe now.

Chick gripped Beau's arm. "We got here in plenty of time, Beau. Let's get her back to the house."

"Right, of course. I know it. I just...if anything happens to her..." Beau seemed to recover himself. He turned back to Felicity and spoke quietly. "I'm going to see how cold you've gotten." He unzipped her coat and gently reached beneath her clothes to put his hands on her waist.

Felicity wondered if she should say something or slap his hands away, but she trusted Beau. Besides, she couldn't find the strength to lift her hands. He unzipped her slacks and Felicity felt his gentle hands moving over her hips.

Now she started to react. "Beau, don't . . . you can't . . ." She pushed clumsily at his hands.

Her delayed reaction brought the ghost of a smile to Beau's tight lips. "Her skin is warm all over," he said to Chick. "You're right. We got here in time."

He lifted Felicity to her feet. As the light hit her face, he swore viciously. "Chick, look at her face!"

"Stop it," Felicity demanded. "Stop talking about 'her.' Talk to me." She tried to stamp her foot, but her leg was so stiff from cold that it almost buckled under her.

Beau's horrified stare was riveted on Felicity's cheeks.

"Oh, don't worry about that." She chewed a moment on her lips to make them move more naturally. "My face stopped hurting ages ago. Before I found the shed, I think." As she spoke, Felicity touched her cheeks, but she couldn't feel her fingers at all. She pushed harder and still felt nothing.

Beau grabbed her hand and pulled it away from her cheeks. "Don't touch your face, Felicity."

His alarmed tone struck fear in her heart. "What's wrong?" she cried. "Why can't I feel anything? Beau, tell me, please!"

Felicity's rising panic seemed to calm Beau, though the strain didn't leave his eyes. "Your cheeks are frostbitten, but not too badly, I hope. It'll just depend on how long they've been frozen. You weren't in here very long, we know that. But the sooner we take care of it the better, so let's get you back to the house."

Felicity wasn't sure what frostbite meant, but Beau's matter-of-fact manner reassured her. Chick opened the door and snow swirled into the shed.

"I can't do it, Beau." Felicity cringed against his chest. "I can't go back out there."

Beau hugged her close. "It's okay, Felicity."

He took off his scarf and wrapped it around her head twice to protect her face from the wind. Blindfolded, she felt Beau's strong arms lifting her and cradling her against his chest. When he stepped outside, Felicity shuddered at the force of the wind and clung to him, wishing she were still asleep. Vaguely, she heard his voice over the howling wind.

"Her face, Chick . . . If anything happens . . ."

Felicity wondered what Beau meant, but she was too relieved at being on her way back to the house to worry about it. When she felt Beau start to climb the back steps, she tried to stand up and walk into the house by herself. At her first movement, his arms tightened around her.

"Hold still, woman," he growled. He carried her into the dining room and deposited her gently on the love seat in front of the fire, propping her head up with pillows.

"Felicity, thank heavens," she heard Alma say, relief in her voice.

"Is Cherry okay?" Felicity mumbled from inside Beau's scarf as she clumsily unwound it.

"Ash got her to take a sleeping pill. He's with her now." Alma gasped at the sight of Felicity's face.

"Mom, get me some soft cloths, water and a thermometer, will you?" Beau said, tugging off Felicity's boots.

"A thermometer?" Felicity asked.

Beau ignored her question as he carefully felt her feet and toes and examined her hands and fingers. He pulled the quilt from the back of the love seat and covered her with it.

"Beau," Felicity said, "I want to look in a mirror."

"No, absolutely not." Beau put his hands on his hips and set his jaw.

Angry at being treated like a child, Felicity flung off the quilt and started to get up. A wry smile broke through the concern on Beau's face as he pushed her back and covered her again.

"I should have known better," he sighed, shaking his head as he handed her a small mirror from the mantel. "But don't say I didn't warn you."

When she looked at her reflection, a strangled gasp broke from her lips. Beau was right—she should never have looked. Her face was a stark cold white, as white as a corpse. Only her lips provided a hint of color, and even they were barely pink. It was a chilling experience to look for herself in the mirror and see this ghostly apparition staring back. Felicity felt a wave of fear clutch her stomach.

"Oh, Beau," she gasped. "I look awful! What does frostbite do? Tell me!"

"If we're in time, it won't do anything," he replied. But the reassuring note in his voice sounded forced. "We'll apply moist heat to your face and your circulation will return. So will your color."

"And if we're not in time?" she heard herself ask in a voice she hardly recognized as her own.

Beau looked sick. He obviously didn't want to answer. "If we're not in time," he said quietly, squeezing her hand, "the circulation won't return to the frostbitten part of your face and . . . and . . ." He turned away from her questioning eyes. "The tissue will die."

Felicity's blood turned to ice water. Mute with horror, she watched Alma carry in a tray holding three bowls, several soft cloths and a thermometer. Beau immediately wet two cloths in the first bowl and placed them lightly to her cheeks.

"This is cool water first, Felicity. Let me know when you feel something." He shook down the thermometer. "Put this under your tongue. I want to see if your internal temperature has dropped."

"Who cares?" Felicity said, jerking her head away and dislodging the cloths.

He patiently remoistened the cloths and put them back on her face. "I could make a few jokes about what I'll do with this thermometer if you don't keep it in your mouth," he said, stroking her hair, "but I guess you're not in a joking mood."

Felicity couldn't be nasty in the face of Beau's compassion, but she wanted to spit out the thermometer. She was terrified. In many ways, this was worse than her panic in the storm. That had seemed like a nightmare. This was very, very real.

Felicity had never thought much about her looks, but this wasn't just a question of being pretty or plain. Now she could become a *freak*: someone people turned away from in the street.

Beau pulled the thermometer from her mouth. "I didn't know you could keep quiet for so long," he said, with a strained smile. "We'll have to keep one of these around all the time." He took two more cloths, dipped them in another bowl and switched them for the cloths on her face. "This water is warmer," he said. "Do you feel anything yet? Anything at all?"

Felicity's mind was as numb as her face; she couldn't answer. She just gazed at Beau, her worried eyes giving him all the answer he needed.

"Well, at least your temperature is normal," Beau said absently. "That means your circulation didn't slow while you were out there."

After dipping cloths in the warmest water, Beau put them on Felicity's face. He softly massaged her cheeks to see if any sensation had returned. Felicity thought she felt a stab of pain from the gentle pressure of his fingertips.

The flash in her green eyes did not go unnoticed by Beau. "What happened, Felicity?"

Felicity was sure now. The numbness in her cheeks was rapidly being replaced by a stinging burn. She felt weak from the tremendous relief. But it hurt!

"Oooo, ouch," Felicity cried, snatching the cloths from her face. "That's too hot."

"Good," Beau said, firmly replacing the cloths, his face softening with relief. "Too hot is perfect. Just perfect."

"Beau, that hurts," Felicity complained as she tried to turn away from the warm cloth Beau was relentlessly holding to her smarting cheeks. Instead of soft fabric, it felt like red-hot sandpaper.

"Some people," Beau muttered with a broad smile, "are never satisfied. A little while ago you were too cold, remember? Now hold still and we'll try one more."

As Beau placed the fresh cloth on her face, Felicity sucked in her breath. "Just my luck," she said wincing, "to be rescued by a sadist."

A glint of irritation lit Beau's dark eyes. "Lucky is right," he snapped. "You're lucky I'm just warming up your beautiful face. I ought to wring your beautiful little neck. You scared us to death, Felicity. Why in the name of all that's holy did you leave the porch?"

Bossy cowboy, Felicity wanted to yell at him. Why did he always get mad at her when she got hurt? "I had to find you. Cherry needed Ash. She was hysterical."

Beau removed the cloths and his rough fingers stroked her cheeks with incredible gentleness. "Soft Eastern skin," he murmured. "And a soft Eastern brain to go with it. How did you think you were going to find us when you couldn't see three feet in front of you? Don't you *ever* do what you're told?"

Felicity indignantly pushed his hand away and sat up, combing her tousled hair with her fingers. "I'm not stupid, Beau. I thought ... I ..." She looked into his eyes and had to swallow hard. Beau's irritation was gone, and his tender look flustered her. "I thought I saw the sled," she finished lamely. She gazed at the crackling fire. "How'd you find me?"

"Mom was out on the porch waving frantically when we came by. She told us you were out in the storm looking for us." Beau raked a hand through his hair. "I have to admit I was a little frantic myself. Luck was with you, though. You found the one building we have wired with an alarm."

"A burglar alarm?" Felicity giggled. "In dangerous downtown Bondurant?"

"Go ahead and laugh, Easterner," Beau said. "It saved your life."

"What on earth . . ."

"It's not a burglar alarm," he said. "It goes off when the door isn't closed tight. If the door's left open in the winter, none of the equipment will start. When the alarm went off today, we knew right where you were. Thank heavens."

"Thank heavens," she agreed, shuddering at the memory of that cold shed.

Beau cupped her chin and she lost herself in the inky blue depths of his eyes. She drew a shaky breath, her heart pounding.

"Promise not to do anything silly while I'm gone this time?" Beau's deep voice was soft.

Felicity's stomach flip-flopped. "You're leaving for the ridge?" She sympathized with Cherry wholeheartedly now. She'd have hysterics herself if it would keep Beau out of that storm.

"Yep."

"Beau." Felicity gazed at him, wanting to take his tired face between her palms. "I want to go with you."

Beau threw up his hands. "Good grief, woman!" he roared. "After what you've just been through, you want to go back out in that storm?"

Felicity looked out the window at the howling flurries of snow and shuddered. "No," she replied. "But I want to go with you anyway."

Her fingers crept to her cheeks, now mildly tingling. Even the horror of frostbite suddenly seemed preferable to staying home alone, imagining Beau lost in the storm as she had been.

Beau's hands clenched into fists. "Well, you're not going, so forget it!" His blue eyes sparked. "At the risk of setting off one of your childish, liberated explosions, I am *ordering* you not to set foot outside this house while I'm gone."

Ordering? Felicity's anger flared, too. "Oh you are, are you?" she snapped. "You can't tell me what to do, you big ape! I'll go wherever I want!"

She stood and tried to shove him aside, but he didn't budge. She ducked around him to reach for her coat, which was thrown across the back of a chair. He grabbed her wrist and spun her around to face him.

"I don't think you heard what I said," he growled, his voice low as his fingers tightened around her slender wrist. "You're not leaving this house." He took a long deep breath and let it out noisily. "Why the devil would you even want to?"

Held so close to Beau that his hot breath stirred the hair at her temple, Felicity couldn't think. "Don't you know what happens to us?" she demanded. "To Cherry? To me? Can't you understand what it's like sitting around waiting to find out if someone you love is dead?" Her words startled her, but as soon as they were out, she knew they were true.

All the anger left Beau's face. Felicity looked down at her hands, suddenly too shy to meet his eyes. He loosened his grip on her wrist and his thumb began to gently massage her wildly beating pulse. Then he buried his hands in her hair and tilted her head. When their eyes met, she saw that his were laughing and serious at once.

"Felicity, listen to me." His voice deepened as he caressed her hair. "Nothing is going to happen to me. I know exactly what I'm doing. I'm a rancher going to feed cows, something I do every day of my life. The added risk from the storm and the distance is much less than you think."

Beau sounded so strong and sure of himself, and the movements of his hands were so persuasive, that Felicity began to relax.

"But if you were to come along and I had to worry about you the whole time, the risk would be much greater—for all of us." He gave her neck a gentle squeeze. "So stay here and keep the home fires burning."

Her fingers curled till her nails carved half-moons in her palms. "Stop saying that!" she cried. "There must be more for women to do here than tend fires. No wonder Cherry wants to leave. You can't keep us all locked in the house forever, you know."

A muscle twitched in Beau's cheek. "I don't have time for any more of this," he said. "If you don't stay inside, I'll..."

Felicity tried to turn away, but Beau's grip on her hair held her fast, so she leaned forward and kissed him. She meant only to give him a little peck, but as her lips tasted his, her love flamed and the kiss consumed her.

Long before she was ready, Beau pulled away and shook his head at her. A helpless smile crinkled the laugh lines around his eyes.

"If I don't stay inside, you'll what?" Felicity breathed.

Beau sighed deeply. "I don't have time for this, either, I'm sorry to say. But I'll be back." He held her away from him and looked at her suspiciously. "Give me your word you'll stay inside, Easterner."

"Of course I will," Felicity said, tracing the deep dimples in his cheeks with her fingers. "I'm easy to persuade."

"Easy?" Beau's severe face crumpled into laughter. "Easy!"

He pressed her fingertips to his lips and left the room, still laughing heartily. The warm rich sound floated in to her from the mudroom. Then the back door slammed and he was gone.

Felicity tried to ignore the aching emptiness Beau left behind him, but the whole house echoed with it. She gazed into the fire, listening to the clock on the mantel tick away the minutes. How many would have to tick away before Beau was with her again?

The fire popped and crackled, sending a shower of sparks up the chimney. Felicity warmed her hands over the blazing logs, trying to understand what had happened to her. How could she possibly be in love with Beau? He was so infuriating—domineering and stubborn! But he was also lovable, gentle, tenderhearted. And passionate, her body reminded her with a warm rush. Somehow the storm and her close call with death had made her face feelings that might otherwise have taken her months to recognize.

A sudden thought struck Felicity, and she dropped onto the love seat, her heart fluttering. What if Beau didn't want her? He'd been so tender this afternoon that she'd just assumed her feelings were returned, but he hadn't said anything about love. What if he'd simply felt guilty about her frostbite?

After all, he'd known her only a few weeks. The life-threatening experiences that had made Felicity's feelings so clear to her were just part of Beau's everyday experience. Last night in the barn, he'd stopped their lovemaking. Had he done that because he didn't love her? And this morning, when she'd wanted to return to their bed of straw, Beau had pulled her out into a blizzard.

If only he were here now, beside her, caressing her...then she'd know. Drawing a deep, shuddering breath, Felicity looked at the clock again and wanted to scream.

The storm was teaching her more about life in Wyoming than she'd have learned in months of sunshine. Storms like this one happened all winter here, and Beau would go out in them day after day, while she waited alone.

That awful night in the hospital waiting room rose in her mind again. Was that what her love would sentence her to? Day after day of wondering whether Beau was alive or dead? Felicity groaned inwardly and dragged her eyes away from the white fury outside the window. What a time to fall in love. What a man to fall in love with!

Alma entered the room with an armful of logs. Felicity was so glad to have some company, she almost hugged her.

"How's Cherry?" she asked as Alma added a log to the fire.

"She'll sleep the rest of the day, and through the night, I hope." Alma sat down beside her. "Your cheeks look fine, Felicity. I'm sorry you had such a terrifying experience. I should have known better than to send you out in this storm."

"What about Beau and Ash?" Felicity clenched her fists. "Don't you worry when they go out in a storm like this?"

"They know what they're doing," Alma said with reassuring calm. "They'll be back without mishap, I'm sure, just as always."

"Didn't you ever worry about your husband?" Felicity asked. "Even when you were first married?"

"Oh my, yes." Alma smiled at her memories. "I grew up in Boston. I'd never seen a cow or a horse up close until I came to Wyoming. I was even nervous in the summer—those big animals didn't look a bit safe to me."

"How did you get over it?" Felicity asked enviously.

"Don't you know, Felicity," Alma said, her eyes twinkling like her son's. "It's love that makes us afraid for our men. I realized if I wanted a life without worry, then I had to choose a life without Daniel, and that was something I couldn't even imagine doing. Besides, he came home safely so many times, I began to know he would again. And so will Beau today."

Felicity flushed and looked away. Was it so obvious that she was in love with Beau? She hoped Alma couldn't see how much this conversation had flustered her.

Still, she felt comforted by the older woman's words. "Will they be home for dinner?" she asked.

Alma patted her hand. "I doubt they'll be home that early. Not after . . . well, finding you slowed them down some."

Felicity's shoulders sagged. Beau had saved her from her stupid mistake, and it had put his own life in jeopardy.

When Alma went to her office to work, Felicity got out her files, but she couldn't concentrate. She found herself reading without comprehension, getting up periodically to replenish the fire. She almost laughed at herself. All she'd accomplished the whole afternoon was just what Beau had asked—keep the home fires burning.

Finally at seven o'clock, she went and knocked on Alma's door. "Shouldn't they be back?" she burst out. "Isn't there something we can do?"

"Not you, too, Felicity?" Alma smiled resignedly as she reached for the phone. "Well, I suppose it won't hurt to call the sheriff."

Felicity paced the small room while Alma talked.

"Dusty will go check on them," Alma said when she hung up. "He's an old friend and he understands."

Felicity went back to gazing blindly at her papers, listening to the clock tick away her hope. Alma's strength reminded her of her own mother, who had never for a moment given in to despair during the long recovery from her stroke. Felicity wished she could find the same courage in herself.

By nine o'clock, Felicity's hope was gone. She felt a vise slowly closing on her chest. She was sure that Beau was dead and she had helped to kill him.

She now understood all too well why Cherry couldn't live here. After today, Felicity was sure she couldn't live here, either. For the last eight hours, her heart had been held hostage. It was an experience she would never willingly repeat.

The thought made her want to cry. She had found the one man in the world made just for her, and now she knew she could never live with him. If he wasn't already dead, his once virile body lying beneath a snowdrift, slowly freezing solid.

The jangling phone sounded unnaturally loud in the silence. Felicity ran to the door of Alma's office, preparing herself to hear the worst. Before this call, at least there had been a glimmer of hope. Now there would be none, ever again. The rest of her life would be only pain and guilt and regret. And leading the list of Felicity's regrets would be last night. Now that it was too late, she wished with all her heart that she had consummated her love with Beau.

Alma hung up and smiled at Felicity with tears in her eyes. Felicity's gaze fixed on Alma's smile and she held her breath, afraid to hope.

"They're fine, Felicity," Alma said, taking her hands. "That was the sheriff's dispatcher. Dusty just got back to the highway and called in on his police radio. They had some trouble on the ridge, that's what took so long. But they're fine, and they'll be home soon."

Felicity's breath left her lungs in a rush. The tension drained from her muscles, leaving her light-headed. She stared openmouthed at Alma, who guided her to a chair as her legs folded under her.

Finally, Felicity found her voice. "When will they get here?"

"The sheriff left them at the highway. It'll take them a while to get the sled home." Alma's smile brightened her face and eyes.

"Alma, you were worried, too, weren't you?" Felicity rose to follow Alma to the kitchen, but her legs still felt like jelly, and she collapsed back into the chair.

"Of course I was, dear. They're my sons," Alma said, patting Felicity's shoulder. "Not as worried as you, though. I've waited out plenty of storms before this. Now you just sit there and pull yourself together while I start the coffee."

It was another long hour before a low roaring noise reached them over the sound of the storm. Felicity ran to the window and saw a light coming slowly up the road. Her whole being filled with joy. For minutes, she couldn't move. Finally she shook herself and ran out to the back porch.

Never had a day passed so slowly, and these last few minutes seemed an eternity. By the time Beau trudged up the back steps with Ash and Mike Weber, Felicity was shivering violently. Beau looked at her, his dark eyes glowing. She gazed back at him, knowing she had never seen anything so beautiful as Beau's exhausted face.

I won't cry, she told herself. *If he doesn't touch me, I won't cry.*

But Beau had no intention of not touching her. He reached out and crushed her against his snow-covered chest. As he lifted her into the mudroom and pushed the door closed with his foot, Ash and Mike slipped into the kitchen. Beau hugged her tightly and stroked her hair as she sobbed out all the tensions of this horrible day.

"I was so scared," she finally managed to choke, loosening her grip on Beau's neck.

"I know," he said, tenderly wiping tears from her cheeks with a callused finger. "I knew you'd think the worst but there wasn't a damn thing I could do about it."

It was heaven to be back in Beau's arms. But Felicity knew he must be tired and hungry, and she tried to swallow her tears. "You need to eat," she said, a shaky smile on her still-trembling lips. "Besides your coat is making me cold."

Beau's arms tightened around her. "Tough it out, woman," he said with a grin, his dark eyes roaming hungrily over her face. "I've been working hard for sixteen hours, and I've earned a little of this."

"You've earned a little food, too," Felicity said, flushing with pleasure. "But if this is what you want, I'll stay here as long as you like."

"I was hoping you'd say that, Felicity." Beau was suddenly very serious. "How about for the rest of your life?"

Felicity's heart began to pound so hard she was sure Beau could feel it. "Beau...I only meant..."

Felicity just wanted to revel in her joy at his safe return. She didn't want to think about the future. Pulling away far enough to unbutton Beau's coat, she squirmed inside it against his chest and turned up her face for a kiss.

Beau's arms felt stiff around her. "You didn't answer my question, Felicity."

"No," she said lightly, ignoring his serious tone, "and I'm not going to until I find out whether your lips got frozen today."

Beau's quick laugh caught at her heart. "All right," he said. "Why am I resisting?"

His hands moved down her back to her hips, and he lifted her into the air until her eyes were level with his. His mouth captured hers in a kiss of such passion that Felicity felt their bodies merging into one loving being. It was just a kiss, but it seemed to wipe away all the pain of the day.

When Beau put her down, her knees buckled beneath her, and his arms quickly encircled her waist once more. Felicity could sense his exhaustion. With a quivering sigh, she released him.

"You need to sit down and eat," she said, "and I want to hear what happened. Were you in any danger?"

"Not exactly," Beau answered.

"That's not very informative, Beau." Felicity cocked her head at him, trying to catch his eye.

Beau grinned and ran a weary hand through his damp hair. "I'll tell you everything, Officer, as soon as I get something to eat."

Felicity watched Beau remove his outer clothing, relieved to have steered the conversation onto safer ground. He was asking for a commitment she simply couldn't make—not now, probably not ever. She was quite sure she couldn't live in this harsh country, even to be with Beau. Those awful hours of anguish and terror today had convinced Felicity that she should run from this wonderful man as fast as her legs, and the nearest airplane, could carry her.

Beau leaned against the wall to pull off his boots, his thigh muscles flexing beneath his jeans. Felicity couldn't take her eyes off him. She didn't think she could ever love Beau less than she did at this moment. But the way she felt about his home was something else again. She didn't want to rush into something she couldn't live with, just because she was so glad to see Beau alive. Just because she loved him so much...

Beau regarded her closely, the half smile twitching at his lips. "Are you through arguing with yourself, Easterner?"

Felicity was disconcerted. "Why do you always know what I'm thinking?" she demanded.

"You think too loud."

Felicity laughed and started into the kitchen, but Beau pulled her back. His hands rested heavily on her shoulders as he looked into her eyes. Something in his gaze frightened her. He was so intense. There was none of the humor she had come to expect. She wasn't ready for this.

"Is that swallow of soup you took at lunch all you've eaten all day?"

"I had breakfast with you, Beau," she murmured.

"You must be hungry." He was so close, his earthy masculine smell seemed to envelop her.

"Starved," she whispered, unable to stop the tremor in her voice.

"And you think it's too soon for this, don't you?" His thumb stroked along her collarbone and came to rest on the pounding pulse at the hollow of her throat.

Felicity pushed her hands against his chest as if by holding him away she could stop his words. "Yes, I do," she said earnestly, feeling his breathing quicken with her own. "I'm not ready, Beau, and I don't think you're ready, either."

"This morning I would've agreed with you. But not anymore." He placed a finger firmly on her lips to silence her objections. "This afternoon, when I thought I might have lost you forever, I nearly went out of my mind. Tonight, when I drove up and saw you out there waiting for me, I knew I'd never be glad to get home again if you weren't here. I love you, Felicity. I want you with me, forever."

Felicity could hear every beat of her racing heart. Her eyes saw only Beau. She'd been waiting all afternoon to hear those words, and now she couldn't respond.

Beau moved closer. Felicity felt snaps and zippers pushing into her back as he leaned against her, pinning her to the wall of coats. Ever so slowly his big hands moved down her arms, his touch heating her skin from her shoulders to her fingertips.

His gaze never left her eyes as he lowered his mouth to hers, teasing her lips with feathery touches until she was hungry with wanting him, her whole being begging for his touch. Felicity had never had such feelings, never known such a wanton part of her existed. But she was suddenly sure that it had always been there, inside her—wanting, waiting, *aching* for the right man to bring it out.

Beau's hands were gentle, caressing. Then he, too, seemed to lose an inner battle, and passion inflamed him. His mouth grew demanding. The room began to spin, then, and Felicity closed her eyes, closed her mind, to all but the pulsing pleasure flowing over her. Beau's hands dropped to the back of her thighs and started a tantalizing journey up her legs, over the roundness of her hips. He pulled her willing softness against him, making her achingly aware of how much he wanted her. His need united with hers in a blaze of desire beyond her wildest imaginings.

A fevered moan broke from Felicity's lips, opening her mind to her surroundings. Was she going to find total feminine fulfillment—*here*? On a pile of dirty down coats and soggy mittens? Where three unlocked doors might open any moment to admit Ash or Mike or, worse yet, Alma?

But Felicity was helpless, the flame of her passion cooled not one whit by such misgivings. She clung to Beau with all the desperation this day had roused in her, wanting to merge herself with him, to feel the power of his manhood.

Beau sensed the change in her and lifted his head. Felicity's eyes sought his and found in them the answer to a prayer. Darkened to an inky blue, filled with love, they gazed openly back at her, glowing with the unquenched desire that throbbed between them. Despite the violence of his passion, there was no violence in this man. He knew, they both knew, that he could make love to her, here and now. The resistance she felt was feeble. But Beau had felt it for her, through her, and not made her voice it.

"Too much too fast?" he whispered hoarsely.

"Mmm," she murmured, "like a rocket."

He smiled, his lips quivering. "Not a great place for a date, either." A long deep breath left his lungs. "I think you mentioned dinner?"

Felicity's pounding heart made her voice shaky. "Beau, I can't stand—"

"Can't stand dinner? You need to eat, Felicity."

She began to giggle helplessly. "No, no," she gasped. "I can't stand *up*."

She slid down the wall as Beau gently lowered her to the floor, his own laughter mingling with hers. Ash found them there minutes later—leaning against each other in the tangle of discarded coats, laughing gently at their own private joke.

CHAPTER TWELVE

A COMFORTABLE QUIET filled the warm kitchen as the men ate. Felicity just toyed with her food, never taking her eyes from Beau. Her relief that he was here, safe with her, overcame her hunger. Even Alma's gaze lingered fondly on her sons.

Felicity was dying to know what had happened on the ridge, but didn't want to disturb the tranquillity of the meal. These men had earned their moments of peace. Finally, sipping a cup of coffee laced with brandy, Beau leaned back and raised his heavy-lidded eyes to Felicity.

"How'd you keep quiet for so long, Easterner?" he asked, the half smile slanting his lips.

Felicity's heart pounded as she lost herself in his warm eyes. "What happened?" she asked, hoping her quavery voice didn't make her feelings obvious to everyone at the table.

Beau let his long body slump in the chair. "Murphy's Law."

"Are you sure you want to know?" Mike asked. "It's awfully dull."

"Of course we do," said Alma. "Now stop fooling around and tell us!"

Mike Weber was a large stocky man. His hair was streaked with gray and his sad brown eyes reminded Felicity of a cocker spaniel she'd had as a child. "Ladies," he said, shaking his head. "They always want to know exactly where you've been. As if we'd been out on the town or something.''

Felicity's slender fingers tugged irritably at a curl on her cheek. ''My, you're all being evasive,'' she said, wondering what was such a big secret.

''We got sort of stuck,'' said Ash, giving Alma a quick smile.

''That's it?'' Felicity demanded. ''That's the whole story?''

Beau tilted his chair onto its back legs and regarded the others with a knowing grin. ''If you two think we're going to get out of here without a blow-by-blow description of this whole day, you're dreaming. And I need some sleep.'' He brought his chair down with a bang. ''So tell 'em, Ash. I'll see you in the morning.''

''Beauregard DuBois,'' Alma said with an edge to her voice, ''you stop that clowning this minute! A guest in my house has asked you a civil question. Now for heaven's sake, answer it.''

Beau reached to give Alma's shoulder a squeeze. ''We just don't want you to worry, that's all.''

Alma twisted a napkin through her fingers. ''Not knowing is even worse, Beau.''

''There's a tree down across the road right at the top of the hill.'' Beau's voice was noncommittal. ''The road's real narrow there, and with the wind the way it's been, there's a huge drift against the tree. We were only a few feet from the pasture, but there was no way to get around the drift.''

Alma's knuckles were white around her coffee mug. ''But surely the Cat could get over the drift?''

''Of course it could,'' Beau said. ''So could the sled. But the hay couldn't. Every time we tried to get the sled over, we dumped all the hay. Then we had to reload and try again. The third time we lost the stack, we used the Cat to smash the drift as much as we could before we bothered to reload. The next time, we got over.''

Ash laid his hand over Alma's. "After we got over, it only took us about an hour to feed."

"How long did it take to reload three times?" Alma asked.

"You mean including the time we wasted swearing at the sled and the Cat and the drift and the gods?" Mike Weber's gravelly voice took some of the tension out of the room, and Alma smiled at him.

Ash snorted. "We were pretty fast, considering we had no equipment, the bales were all over the place, and we were fighting that—" he waved his arm toward the window "—every step of the way."

Beau drained the coffee from his mug. "It took four or five hours. But it would have taken longer if you hadn't called Dusty, Mom." He looked up at Alma's worried face. "He and his kid showed up and helped us load the last time, so it went a lot faster."

"But not fast enough," said Ash, rubbing the back of his neck. "I was beat. Still am. I'm glad Cherry stayed in bed."

Alma closed her eyes and pressed her fingertips hard against her temples. Felicity wondered if she was imagining her sons and her friend trudging back and forth in a blinding snowstorm, carrying hay bales until they were ready to drop. Felicity herself couldn't even imagine it; she was just glad it was over.

Alma looked up. "You should all be in bed."

"We're too tired to move," said Ash.

"Nonsense." Alma stood. "Come on, Mike. I'll show you where to sleep." She led him out of the room.

Ash yawned and stretched. "If I had the strength to stand up," he said tiredly to Beau, "I'm sure I could make it to bed."

"Would it help," Beau asked in mock politness, "if I kicked the chair out from under you?" He extended a muscular leg toward Ash's chair.

Ash jumped up. "I can take a hint," he said, grinning. "'Night, Felicity."

Beau rested his chin on his hands and gazed dreamily at Felicity. Exhaustion had softened his features, and his half-closed eyes were more appealing than ever. Felicity desperately wanted to go to him and rub his tired shoulders, kiss his drooping lids. But she stayed in her chair, unsure how to handle all her feelings for him.

"You were in danger, weren't you?" Felicity wondered why she asked. Did she only want confirmation of something she already knew—that her fears today hadn't been groundless? Or did she really hope he would tell her she'd had nothing to fear?

"Some," said Beau. "But what's life without a little danger?"

Felicity clasped her hands tightly together to keep from reaching out for him. "It was my fault," she said, her eyes filling with tears. "You were late because of me."

Anger abruptly hardened Beau's features. "That's drivel! You were just trying to help. Besides, that drift was there all day—you had nothing to do with how long we were gone."

"But if you'd been working during the day..." Felicity began.

Beau reached across the table and took her chin in his hand. "No, Felicity," he said firmly. "It was our own fault for starting out too late. Tomorrow we'll let the hands feed here, and we'll—"

"Tomorrow?" Fear jolted through Felicity like an electric shock, and she pulled away from Beau's caressing fingers. "You're not going back up there tomorrow?" She stood, knocking over her chair, and slowly backed away. Beau tried to take her hands, but she snatched them away. "Don't touch me!" she cried.

Beau stilled his hands but his intense gaze held her. "I thought you understood why Mom was so upset. Do you think she'd be worried about us if the job was finished?"

"I don't understand anything about this place!" Felicity's voice rose shrilly and she pounded on Beau's chest. "Why didn't you leave enough food for two days?"

"We couldn't, Felicity." Beau grabbed her fists and held them tightly against his chest. "If we left too much food, most of it would be trampled and buried under snowdrifts. Besides, we only have one Cat, so we couldn't haul enough for two days."

He moved closer. Freeing her hands, Felicity began to back away again. Her joy at Beau's safe return had made her forget her resolution to run from him and his harsh life. Now all the pain of this afternoon came rushing back, and Felicity knew that pain would never end as long as she stayed with Beau. She wished she could leave right this minute before she ever had to face another day like today. The log wall against her back stopped her retreat. Beau walked slowly toward her as if he didn't want to frighten her away. He put his hands on the wall behind her shoulders, pinning her between his arms, and looked deeply into her green eyes.

"Felicity." His voice was rough with hurt. "Why are you running away? This afternoon you said you loved me. Didn't you mean it?"

Felicity drew a long shuddering breath. She wanted to hide, to disappear, to do anything to avoid this declaration. But when she looked up into Beau's velvety eyes, she couldn't refuse him the truth.

"I do love you, Beau," she said helplessly. "I love you so much it makes my heart hurt."

Hope and desire flared in his eyes. He leaned toward her, his breath warming her lips. Felicity felt trapped, pinned against the wall by his arms and her love.

"I love you, too, Felicity. More than I can say." His lips moved slowly across her cheek, his words soft in her ear.

Felicity shook her head. "You don't know me."

"I know all I need to—I know how much I love you. I've
waited my whole life to feel this way. I'd begun to think I
never would." He nibbled softly on her earlobe. "As soon
as I met you, I knew you were different...special. But
watching Ash and Cherry's marriage... Well, it took me a
while to admit I could feel this way about an Easterner."

Beau's strong arms enfolded her and lifted her, as his face
nuzzled her tousled curls. Cradling her close, he pushed
through the door and carried her down the hall. Drowning
in waves of love and desire, Felicity pressed her lips against
his bristly jaw, reveling in the prickly feel of his whiskers.
She wrapped her hands tightly around him, her fingers tangling in his hair, longing to be even closer, yet wishing deep
down that she was far away.

Beau switched on the light in her room with his elbow and
laid her on the bed. Placing a hand on either side, he leaned
over her. She was mesmerized by his presence. Breathing
shallowly through her slightly parted lips, her whole being
softened with female welcome. The heat from his body
warmed hers; his breath against her cheek smelled of coffee
and brandy. His eyes were darker than she'd ever seen them,
deep and warm and loving. Every cell of her was alive with
the need to touch him, to feel him touching her.

But she knew if he touched her now, she would be consumed by passion. She wouldn't stop this time, no matter
what Beau said. And when their love was consummated,
she'd never be able to leave. She'd be trapped here forever
in this frozen wilderness—hating it, hating every minute of
it until she and Beau hated each other.

No! She couldn't make love to Beau, but she hadn't the
strength to tell him. She felt as if she were on the edge of an
abyss, slipping. Stiffening, she pressed down into the bed,
afraid to move.

Beau sensed her doubts. A questioning look formed in the
depths of his dark eyes. "Felicity, why are you scared? I

won't hurt you. I'd never force you to do something you didn't want to do."

"Force!" Felicity almost laughed but it turned into a sob.

She pulled Beau down to her, feeling desire throbbing through her misery. How could she possibly leave this man she loved so much? But how could she live with him in constant fear? She buried her face in his chest, wetting his shirt with her tears.

Beau rolled over onto his side and turned her toward him. She tried to keep her face hidden, but he drew back to look into her eyes. One finger softly wiped the tears from her cheek.

"It's okay, Felicity. I can wait. I've waited thirty-four years to find you. We have our whole lives to love each other."

Felicity pulled away from Beau and sat up. She hadn't wanted to confront this, not now, not ever. She'd almost rather let Beau think she hated him than have him find out what a coward she was.

He sat up and slipped his arm around her shoulders, cuddling her close. "I tried not to love you, you know. I tried to convince myself that all I felt for you was desire. Every morning when you walked into the dining room, I felt like I'd been kicked in the stomach, I wanted you so much. But I kept reminding myself you were an Easterner, a real estate developer of all things, and that it could never work between us. But today, when I thought I'd lost you . . ." He looked down at her, impaling her with his piercing gaze. "Felicity, I've never loved anyone so much in my life."

"You were right the first time, Beau." Felicity took his face between her palms. "It won't work. Look at Cherry and Ash. They're both miserable."

Beau's fingers dug into her shoulders. "Don't say that!" he said fiercely. "You're not Cherry. You're different. You're willing to try things. Look what you did today, going out in the storm to help her."

Felicity winced at the pressure of his hands. "It's this storm that's convinced me I can't live here," she said sadly. "I'd be a prisoner of my fears all winter. I can't go through another day like today. No matter how much I love you." Her voice caught in her throat. "Because I love you so much. Because there will always be days like today. I can't sit home all winter waiting to hear that you're dead. I can't. I'll never stop loving you, but I can't live like that."

"You're just not used to it."

"You won't even *try* to understand!" Felicity cried, shoving his hands away. "What would you say if I asked you to move to Florida?"

"You really are a dude, aren't you?" Beau stood up and glowered at her, his fists planted firmly on his hips. "You'd throw away our love because of a little snow."

"A *little* snow!" Felicity exclaimed. "Why you . . . you stubborn cowboy. Just because you want to sit in the middle of nowhere and freeze your—"

Beau grabbed her shoulders and shook her. "Easterner!"

"That's right." Felicity pressed her fingertips to her eyes. "The East is my home. It's close to my family. Even if I could learn to live with your harsh life, I could never move that far from my parents. What if Mom has another stroke? They need me."

"It sounds like you need them." The pain in Beau's eyes stabbed at her. "I thought you were a woman, Felicity. But I see you're still a girl."

The disappointment in his voice made Felicity's stomach clench. "I'm woman enough to know our marriage wouldn't work," she snapped. "Isn't it better to find out now? I know this ranch is your life. I'd never ask you to leave it. But you can't expect me to leave my life, either."

"We could make it work."

"How? Will you make changes, too?" Felicity looked at him appraisingly. "Will you stay home with me tomorrow, Beau? All day?"

"Felicity, use your head!" Beau threw up his hands. "I'm a rancher. Ask me something possible."

"That's just what I mean," she said, jabbing a finger toward him. "You won't accept my life at all. But you want me to..." Her voice drifted to a halt as she realized the enormity of what she was about to say.

Beau sat next to her on the bed. "That's right, Felicity," he said, his voice deeply serious. "That's exactly what I'm asking." He put his fingers under her chin and tipped up her face. He placed a kiss on her mouth, his lips gently massaging hers. "I'm asking you to share my life. I've never wanted anything so much." His hot breath feathered the silky hair at her temples. "But I'm not sure you're ready. You'll have to grow up first."

"Oh, Beau," Felicity gasped against his mouth. She wrapped her arms around his neck, her lips seeking his.

"C'mon, Easterner," he said, trying to gently pull away. "We need some sleep. I do, anyway. I won't give up this easily, but we can talk again tomorrow. At least I know you won't run away from me in this storm."

"Will I see you in the morning?" Felicity clung to him. "What time are you leaving?"

"Early. Much too early for you to bother getting up." Beau took her hands from behind his neck and held them firmly in her lap. "I'll see you at lunch."

"No, Beau, please," she said, ineffectively tugging at his hands. "I couldn't stand it if I didn't say goodbye to you. Please."

Beau's half smile curved his lips as he shook his head at her. "You still don't believe we're coming back, do you? All right, you silly Easterner, I'll come in and say goodbye in the morning. But don't get up. It'll be before dawn and you need to sleep."

Felicity felt the pressure of Beau's fists against the mattress as he started to stand up. Would she ever see him again? She felt a flash of panic.

"Beau," she said, her breath coming quickly, "don't leave." She put her hands on his hard-muscled shoulders to bind him to her, suddenly unwilling to let him go.

Beau resisted her pressure. "No, Felicity. I can't make love to you like this." A deep sigh shook his body. "Heaven knows I want to. I want to make love to you now and tomorrow and every day for the rest of my life. I want to wake up every morning and see you next to me on the pillow. But I don't want a one-night stand and neither do you. It would hurt us both too much."

He kissed her on the forehead and settled her on the pillows. With a last look of longing, he left the room.

Felicity wanted to call out to him, to beg him to stay with her. Silently, she watched the door close behind his broad back, her body aching with loss.

FELICITY HEARD NOISES in the hall and forced her eyes open. It couldn't be morning yet; the window still looked black. She rolled over to go back to sleep and saw Beau tiptoeing through the door in his stocking feet.

Felicity stretched under the comforter, trying to wake up. "Beau?" she murmured, still foggy with sleep.

His hand rested on her waist, holding her down. "Don't get up, Felicity."

She felt the mattress tilt as Beau sat down. Her body was drawn to him, as if of its own accord. She curled her legs lazily around him, nuzzling her head against his hard thigh, wondering if she was dreaming him. "Mmm, Beau, I love you."

The scent of his after-shave drifted down to her, and she reached up to stroke his smooth cheek. Her sleep-warmed body glowed with the heat of his nearness. Her hand trailed around to caress the back of his neck, urging him closer.

Without opening her eyes, she pressed her lips to the hollow of his throat and grazed the tender skin below his ear with kisses. As her lips brushed across his cheek, she heard him moan and then his mouth claimed hers. She gasped with pleasure as Beau's thrusting tongue tangled with hers. Felicity pulled him closer, pushing her swelling breasts against his hard chest.

"Felicity." Her name was a groan on Beau's lips as he pulled away. "No, love, we can't. When you leave, we'll both regret it."

Leave? Felicity tried to rouse her brain to understand what Beau meant. How could she possibly leave Beau? Her resolve of the night before, her fears of the storm, were lost in some part of her mind that wasn't yet awake. In her half-sleeping state all she could think of was how desperately she loved Beau. With him, she heard the bells she had waited so long to hear. Of course she'd never leave him.

Beau still held her away from him but his hands moved from her shoulders to her elbows, gently massaging, as if he couldn't bear to let her go. The warmth from his body and the heat in hers overwhelmed her. Gazing into his melting eyes, Felicity slowly unbuttoned the neck of her nightgown, letting the bodice fall open. Her eyes stayed locked with Beau's as he groaned at the sight of her breasts.

"Felicity, I love you." His fingers tightened fiercely around her arms. "Don't you know what you're doing to me?"

Somewhere in the dim recesses of her mind, Felicity, too, wondered at herself. But the thought was lost as she stared into Beau's loving eyes. His gaze traveled over her like a flame, and she quivered in anticipation.

As if in a trance, Beau slowly circled her breasts, one after the other, with gentle fingers. Felicity groaned at the aching love and the passion consuming her. Somehow all her fears for Beau's safety, even the buried realization that she would have to leave him, made her love more intense.

She reached up to open his shirt, wanting to feel his skin against hers. As her fingers trailed across his hard flat stomach, his muscles tightened under her touch.

"I love you so much, Felicity," he groaned, as he lowered his heated body over hers. "Are you sure..."

"Love me, Beau," she breathed. "Love me...."

IN THE WARM AFTERGLOW of their lovemaking, Beau stroked the damp hair from her brow. "Felicity, sweetheart," he murmured, raining kisses on her face, "I'm sorry I had to hurt you."

"It didn't hurt, Beau. It was...it was..." She buried her face in his shoulder, blushing.

"You silly female," he said tenderly. "How can you be bashful after that?"

She snuggled into the crook of his arm, and he gathered her against his chest. "Isn't this better than feeding a bunch of cows?" she sighed.

Beau's arm stiffened. "I still have to feed the cows."

She draped her leg across his. "You can't leave me now, Beau," she said, smiling. "*I'd* freeze to death."

Beau frowned at her. "Felicity, the cows won't stop eating just because we made love."

"I don't see why not." She ran a finger along his jawline. "I'd stop eating for love." Her thumb traced his full lower lip. "Make love to me again, and see if I'll skip breakfast. Just this once."

Laughing, Beau moved away from her and sat up. "I wish I could."

Felicity wrapped the quilt around her, shivering from the loss of his warm body. How had she let her sleep-fogged brain persuade her they could work things out? Nothing had changed. He would still go out into the storm, and she would spend the day in agony, wondering if he'd return.

Beau pulled on his jeans and tucked in the long tails of his wool shirt. Despite what had happened, despite what they felt, he was really going to leave her. Stunned, Felicity turned her face away as he sat down on the bed.

"Felicity, I'm late already. I'll be back by lunchtime, you'll see. There's nothing to worry about. We can talk when I get back." Beau stroked her cheek and planted a kiss on her temple. "You'll learn, Easterner. It's only frightening because you aren't used to it."

She rolled over and took his hands. "Beau," she said urgently, "please don't leave me. Not now. Just for today, stay with me. I need you."

Beau looked stricken and clutched her against him. "Do you think I want to leave you? There's nowhere I'd rather be than here with you. You must know that." She tried to twist out of his arms but her strength was no match for his. "I have no choice, Felicity. Wait for me."

He kissed the tears sliding down her cheeks, kissed her quivering lips. Her response was immediate and she moaned as he pulled away.

"See you at lunch, love," he said and was gone before she could speak.

LATE THAT AFTERNOON, Felicity sat in the tiny room Alma called her office. She had gone there to hide from her fears of the storm. She sat at Alma's desk recording calves' births in large black ledger books. It was surprisingly satisfying work, updating these dry records of continuing life.

Hearing Cherry's frightened voice from the dining room, Felicity stared out the window at the ever-present storm. Cherry was calmer today, but Felicity wondered how long that would last if the storm kept up.

Despite a flannel shirt borrowed from Alma and a crackling fire in the wood stove, Felicity felt icy cold. She couldn't block out the image of a snow-covered Beau up on the ridge. He had assured her he would be home for lunch. Now it was four o'clock. She forced her gaze away from the window and continued to work, steeling herself for the worst. Even if Beau returned safely today, Felicity knew she could never survive this kind of ordeal time after time.

When she finally heard the back door slam and Beau's voice raised in greeting, Felicity was shocked to see it was after five o'clock. The intense joy that surged through her left her weak. Briefly, she wondered what had happened to make them late today. But she didn't really want to know.

Now she knew that he was safe, Felicity wasn't eager to face Beau. There were only a few more calves to record, so she picked up the pen once more.

When Beau entered the office, Felicity could feel his presence warming her. She felt his stare, smelled his damp wool and denim, but she kept her eyes glued to the last calf record. The fingers of her left hand ached from gripping the arm of the chair.

"It's great to see you so at home here, Easterner." Beau's muscular thigh filled her vision as he sat down on the desk in front of her. "Is it pretty dull work compared to your job?"

"No." Felicity kept her eyes lowered. "Quite the reverse. But I'm not finished and you're sitting on the last record."

"The last one!" Beau sounded stunned. "Mom said there were more than a thousand births to record. You must be cut out for this work. Don't you think so?"

Felicity noticed a worn spot in the faded denim covering his thigh.

Beau covered her hands. "Look at me, Felicity," he ordered. "You can't hide forever."

She raised pain-filled eyes to him. "You've been out there for twelve hours, Beau. Five hours more than you expected. Is it always like this?"

Beau slipped his hands up her arms to rest reassuringly on her shoulders. "No, it's *never* like this. *We* keep our cows in winter pasture. Believe me, this will never happen again."

"You mean you always come home on time in the winter?" she persisted.

Beau sighed and shook his head. "No, love, I can't promise that. We come home when our work is done, not before."

Felicity gently removed his hands from her shoulders. The tortured look on Beau's face was blurred by her tears. "I know that, Beau. It's why I won't be here waiting. I love you too much, and I'm just not strong enough."

A sob broke from her throat. Beau reached for her, but she pulled out of his arms and fled.

Two DAYS LATER, Felicity sat stiffly in the car next to Beau as they drove through Hoback Canyon toward the airport. The black road snaking ahead between hills of white was almost dry. On each side were deep piles of dirty snow left by the plow.

How different it looked from the beautiful green valley she'd seen when she arrived. The snow disguised hills, mountains and trees; the Hoback River was a roaring muddy torrent. And this was spring! The sun shone warmly, and Felicity could hear the steady drip of snow melting from trees and rocks.

How would this drive look in winter, when the road, too, was white, when skidding cars and dark clouds were the norm? What if she had to make this drive at forty below on black ice in the dead of night to have a baby? To rush an injured husband to the hospital? Felicity shuddered, sure she had made the right decision, sure that back in Florida, away from the terror of the storm and the ever-present reminder of Beau's beloved face, the anguish she felt now at leaving him would diminish.

Feeling Beau's gaze upon her, Felicity turned to him and tried to smile. The pain she saw written on his rugged features took her breath away. The changes outside the car were nothing compared to the changes she felt inside. How wrong she'd been about Beau. When they'd met, she had thought him arrogant and cold. *Cold!*

As she looked at Beau, she knew she should never have let him into her heart. She could return physically to her safe, sunny home and her well-paid job. But her heart would always remain with Beau. In these forbidding mountains where she could never live.

Felicity's hand found Beau's thigh of its own volition. "When did you change your mind about me?" she asked.

"In the truck on the way to the ranch."

"You did not." She stared at him in disbelief. "Why didn't you tell me?"

Beau chuckled. "What should I have said, Easterner?"

"How did you know?"

"Because the mountains made you feel better, took away your anger. I knew then you'd learn to love this place if you'd stay here long enough." He squeezed her hand as he spoke. "I still know that's true. You just haven't stayed long enough."

Felicity sighed sadly. "Maybe I stayed *too* long."

Beau's grip on her hand tightened painfully. "For such a stubborn woman—" his lips twisted into the pretense of a grin "—you're sure giving up easily. You must not want me as much as I want you."

Felicity folded her hands in her lap. She had no answer for Beau. It would be pointless to tell him she wanted him with every fiber of her being. Every word they said made it harder for her to leave.

Felicity and Beau stood in the airport like polite strangers waiting for her plane. Her chin was lifted firmly as she stared straight ahead, afraid to look at the love in his eyes, to let him see the love in hers.

Beau grabbed her shoulder. "Felicity, this is insane." She was startled by the anger in his voice. "You can't walk out of my life this way."

Felicity clamped her trembling bottom lip with her teeth. "Beau, we've been over this a hundred times. You won't stop ranching and I won't get over my fears. I'm just not cut out for this sort of life."

She tried to look away but he pulled her roughly to face him. "Felicity, you've got to grow up sometime. There are risks in every life."

Felicity closed her eyes. "*My* life is safe. I understand it. I know what's going to happen." She glared at him. "I don't spend my days wondering if my loved ones are alive or dead."

"Okay, Easterner." Beau gave her a shake. "Go back to your sheltered little-girl life if you have to, but think about what you're giving up."

"Like you thought about selling the ranch?" Felicity asked, a smile finally lifting the corners of her lips.

Beau rolled his eyes. *"No!"*

"You mean," Felicity said, her shoulders alive to the feel of Beau's now-gentle hands, "not like a stubborn, mule-headed cowboy but like a soft-headed Eastern pushover."

"That's it exactly," said Beau, leaning closer until their lips were almost touching. "Promise, Felicity, promise you'll think about it." His lips brushed hers. "Promise you'll think about me in Florida."

Felicity looked up at Beau through her thick lashes, wondering if she'd ever think about anything else again. She felt herself melting, leaning into his lips. With a start she straightened. This was no time to be kissing Beau.

She shrugged off his hands. "You want me to make all the changes, Beau. You won't listen to my ideas about the lake. You won't even give me that much."

"Hey." Beau held up his hands. "I'm not inhuman. I saw what the storm did to Cherry. I told you yesterday to draw up a proposal to develop the lake and show it to Mom and Ash."

"What about you, Beau? Will you look at it?" Felicity planted a fist on her hip. "With an open mind? It might be the answer for your whole family."

"No, Felicity," Beau admitted, running both hands down his face. "I told you before, I'll never have an open mind about this. I hate the whole idea. But I'll go along with whatever Mom and Ashley decide." He cupped her chin. "And you think about standing on your own two feet and living with the man you were made for."

Felicity gulped as she started backing toward the gate. She had to leave quickly before she began to cry. "I'll call you about the lake."

Beau shook his head. "Call Mom or Ash. I want to hear from you on another subject." He kissed her lips. "Don't wait too long, Felicity."

Felicity couldn't say another word. She turned and fled for the plane, wondering if she would ever see Beau again.

CHAPTER THIRTEEN

FELICITY ADDED the mystery novel to the pile of unfinished paperbacks on her bedside table and turned off the light. As she pulled up the sheet, she wondered if Beau was tossing and turning in bed, too, thinking of tomorrow. The month that had passed since she left Wyoming had been the longest of her life. And now Beau was coming to Florida to meet with Bob Peters, the president of Worldwide Time-Share Inc.

Felicity plumped her pillow and flopped onto her stomach. She ached with a fierce longing to see Beau, yet it was her own choice that his visit tomorrow would be only for business. She rolled onto her back again. How was she going to keep her mind on time-shares with Beau sitting across the table from her?

THE WAITRESS in the restaurant at Tampa International Airport cleared away their nearly untouched plates. "You two didn't eat much dinner," she said. "Dessert?"

Beau shook his head and the waitress left their table. But when Beau turned his eyes on Felicity, the politeness changed to anger, and her stomach lurched.

"We don't get along well in airports, do we, Beau?" She gave him a weak grin.

"It's not the airport, and you know it." His voice held none of the humor she'd missed so much the past month. "I won't be back, Felicity."

Anguish squeezed her heart. She'd been so sure that time away from Beau would dull the pain of leaving him, lessen the intensity of her emotions. As she gazed at him now, she knew that wasn't true. She loved him even more than she had in Wyoming. Every day they'd been apart, her love had grown.

But so had her fears.

"What if we need your input again on the lake development?"

"You didn't need me this time." He took her hand. "Felicity, do you know what I thought when you called me?"

She gripped his fingers as though she was afraid he would slip away. "I told you the truth."

"I couldn't believe you'd ask me to come all this way just to listen to that guff about time-shares." His dark eyes brimmed with the same anguish that filled her heart. "I love you, Felicity. I don't give a damn what you do to the lake."

"But I thought you wanted to know—"

"I told you I'd go along with whatever Mom and Ash decide." His grip on her hand grew tighter. "Since I got here, all we've talked about is business. I won't pretend that's all there is between us. I haven't even kissed you."

Her gaze went naturally to his lips. She longed to feel them on hers, but that was impossible. She forced a quavery laugh. "No, and you're certainly not going to now."

At last a tiny smile crossed his eyes. "Want to bet?"

"Beau, you wouldn't!" she whispered, trying to tug her hand free.

With torturous deliberation, he stood and pulled her to her feet, then kept pulling until her body was pressed against his.

"Beau, stop it!" Felicity struggled helplessly. "Everyone is staring at us!"

His hand on her waist held her against him, while his other hand tangled in her long auburn curls, holding her head immobile. "Then let's give them something to look at."

Heat rushed to her cheeks as Beau's lips descended. She tried to fight the familiar melting sensation, the aching need in her core—but she couldn't. As her lips opened to his, Felicity knew he was right: this was why she had asked him to come.

When he finally released her, Felicity hardly remembered where she was, barely heard the giggles around her. Clutching the back of a chair for support, she watched Beau pick up his Stetson from the table and turn to her. Sliding a hand behind her neck, he looked deeply into her eyes. "Don't call me again, Felicity, until you're ready to be my wife."

Tears blurred her last view of Beau as she watched his long unhurried stride take him out of the restaurant.

To HIDE HER ANGER at Bob Peters, Felicity turned her chair and glared out the big tinted window at Tampa Bay. In the three months since Beau had gone back to Wyoming, arguing with Bob had become her prime occupation. They'd always worked well together in the past, but now he seemed to be going out of his way to be contrary.

Felicity spun her chair back to face him. "No, Bob," she said, determined to stay calm. "You can't pave the lake road. We agreed we'd be especially careful to preserve the natural environment here. Wildnerness is the theme of this development, remember? Not concrete and asphalt."

Scotty grimaced. "Kiddo, I knew you left your heart in Wyoming, but not your head, too."

Felicity glanced at him irritably. "I'm being perfectly reasonable."

"No, you're not," Bob said. "We can't get our equipment up to the lake on a narrow dirt road. We have to cut trees to widen it. That means we need skidders and dozers.

How do you suggest we get the construction equipment up there to build the condos? Airlift it in?''

Felicity glowered at Bob, then at Scotty, who was nodding in agreement, then back out at Tampa Bay. Was she being unreasonable? Alma hadn't seemed to think so the several times Felicity had talked to her since Beau's visit. Of course, no one at the ranch had actually agreed to anything. They were still just listening to Felicity's proposals.

My proposals, my foot, she thought bitterly. These ideas were all Scotty's and Bob's. For weeks Felicity had argued them out of high-rise condos, out of cutting half the trees away from the shoreline to enlarge the beach and even out of having a minimall at one end of the lake with boutiques and specialty shops.

But why was she arguing with them now? She must have known they'd need to widen that narrow twisting road if they were to do any building at the lake. Scotty and Bob were right—she *was* being irrational.

Closing her eyes, Felicity thought about the day Beau had taken her to the lake; remembered the doe and her fawn, the sun sparkling off the icy water, the perfect little beach. Of course that tiny beach wouldn't be big enough for a whole development full of people. But Felicity couldn't be the one to despoil it.

Good heavens, what had happened to her? She knew she'd fallen in love with Beau. But she hadn't realized until this moment that she'd also fallen in love with Wyoming: with *Beau's* Wyoming, just the way it was now, not covered with concrete and plywood.

Felicity blinked, feeling dazed. How could she possibly have lost her heart to the very place that had driven her away from the only man she would ever love? She couldn't live there herself, but she would do everything in her power to protect it from others.

Felicity drew a deep breath, preparing herself for the final showdown. "Bob," she said, "I'm really sorry to have wasted so much of your time. This just isn't going to work. Mrs. DuBois won't sell without my recommendation, and I'm afraid I can't give it.''

A few hours later, Felicity was on her way to her parents' condo, shaken but enormously relieved the battle was over. After alternately shouting and cajoling, beating their fists on her desk and sinking back in their chairs groaning, Bob and Scotty had eventually realized she wouldn't budge and given up. Thank goodness, actual cash outlays had been small, and Scotty had agreed to swallow them.

Felicity pulled the pins from her chignon and opened the sunroof. Her hair cascaded to her shoulders, instantly curling in the warm moist air. Where did she go from here? she wondered. She still had her job but her boss was furious, and she could kiss her partnership goodbye. She still had her business contacts, but they would be leery of her for a while. Worst of all, except for one last phone call to Alma, Felicity had now severed her only remaining link with Beau.

She stopped the car to throw some change into the Bayway tollbooth and continued over the bridge. For the past few months, she admitted now, the only reason she'd pursued this project was to stay in touch with Beau. She hadn't actually talked to him since his disastrous visit. But every time she'd spoken with Alma or Ash, Felicity had felt closer to Beau than she ever would again.

What reason could she dream up for calling him now? Only one, her heart answered, and she still wasn't ready for that. After three months of missing Beau—thinking of him all day and half the night—she was still convinced that living with him through Wyoming winters would ultimately destroy their love.

Not that I'm doing much living without him, Felicity thought ruefully.

As she pulled into the parking lot at her parents' condo, she heard Scotty's parting words echoing in her ears. ''Kiddo, the past few months, you might as well have been in outer space. You drift around like a ghost, with purple circles under your eyes and a permanent frown on your face. You love that cowboy so much you can't work or think or make a rational decision. Now I find out you love his darn countryside, too. Why don't you ship yourself back out there, and I'll visit you in the summer.'' He peered at her over his glasses. "*Is* it ever summer out there?''

Felicity hadn't been able to answer. Scotty couldn't begin to understand how frightened she was of that cold harsh country, how helpless she'd felt there, alone, waiting for Beau, fearing news of his death. Just because she loved the rugged beauty of the place didn't mean she was strong enough to live there.

She entered the elevator, punching the button for the seventh floor, and sighed. This past week she'd barely been able to hide her ennui over Scotty's new shopping mall. Her work had become meaningless; even the lost partnership meant nothing. She'd thought her safe familiar world would soothe her. Instead it bored her. The memory of Mig's newborn colt was much clearer in her mind than this morning's negotiations. Or did her weeks on the ranch just seem more vivid because she'd shared them with Beau?

Her father was sitting at the kitchen table sipping tea and reading the paper. "What's wrong with my favorite girl?'' he asked. "You look like you've been through a wringer.''

"Oh, Dad.'' Felicity sank into a chair. "I don't want to bother you with my troubles. I know how tired you get taking care of Mom.''

Anger flashed across her father's face. "Felicity, when are you going to get it through your head? Your mother's fine. In fact, she's out right now, having dinner with a friend.'' He took another mug from the cupboard, poured boiling water over a teabag and stirred. "Don't you think we know you've been trying to spare us? Something happened with that man in Wyoming that's been upsetting you as much as

Clarissa's stroke." He put the cup in front of her. "Now drink up and tell me about it."

Felicity smiled at him gratefully. It would be a relief to stop pretending that nothing was wrong. Once she started, the words poured out. If the sun hadn't set, she wouldn't even have noticed the passage of time.

"I guess I really needed to talk," she said finally, getting up to turn on the light.

Her father smiled. "I guess you did, sweetheart. Do you want to hear what I think?"

"Of course, I do, Dad," Felicity said. "I've wanted to know for months."

He paused a moment, seeming to choose his words carefully. "I've seen a lot of marriages in my life and most of them have been happy enough. But over the years I came to realize that what your mother and I have is special. Most people never find a love even close to ours." He reached across the table to take his daughter's hand. "But now you've found that rare kind of love, and you're willing to give it up. I can't understand it."

"But, Dad," Felicity cried, "what if he dies? I couldn't live through it."

"Honey," he said, squeezing her hand, "I wish this was as easy as the time you broke your arm falling off your bike. Of course, Beau will die—everyone dies. I hope it won't happen for years and years. When he does, it will be as horrible as you imagine, like your mother's stroke was for me. But so what? If Clarissa and I had only had a few years of marriage before her stroke, it would *still* have been worth it. Think what you're giving up."

Felicity had thought of almost nothing else for the past three months. The pain of being without Beau was worse than she'd ever believed possible. In her heart, she knew it was madness to run away from a love like theirs. But did she have the strength to live in Beau's precarious world—for a chance at happiness that might end any winter day?

Felicity's throat ached with unshed tears. "What about you and Mom? I'd be so far away."

Her father shrugged. "Felicity, that's what happens when children grow up. We can't hold on to you forever, and you can't live your life for your mother. Of course, we'll miss you. But if you let your fears keep you from experiencing all the joy you can with Beau, then we'll have failed as parents."

"Never feel that way, Dad," Felicity said. "You're the best parents anyone could have."

"But not if we can't help you make the right decisions."

Felicity looked out at the dark night sky. The haze of light from the many condos on the island hid the stars. She remembered how brightly the Milky Way had sparkled over her and Beau in Wyoming, and suddenly she knew: her life was there, with him, for as long as it lasted.

When the storms came, she would hide in Alma's little office, where time passed quickly, and work until Beau came back to her. And if one day he didn't return, at least they'd have shared every minute of love they could. Her father and Alma had said almost the same thing—life with Beau might sometimes be hard, but life without the one you loved was unendurable. The decision broke over her like a wave of sanity. How could she have hesitated so long?

Feeling almost breathless with joy, she looked back at her father and pushed her teacup across the table toward him. "Know what I love the most about Beau, Dad?"

"No, what?"

"He makes the most divine coffee and he *never* drinks tea! I've always hated this stuff."

They both stood and hugged each other, laughing and crying. "When Mom gets back, will you tell her I'm getting married?" Felicity asked. "Will you give me away, Dad?"

"Never! Expect us every Christmas and at the birth of every grandchild—dozens, I hope."

Back in her own condo, Felicity sat curled in a corner of the couch, her hand moving hesitantly toward the telephone receiver, then back to her lap. Naturally Beau would be glad to hear she'd canceled the lake development. She glanced nervously at the airplane ticket on the coffee table. Would he be just as glad to hear her decision about him? Maybe she should have waited to buy the ticket. It had been three months. Did he still want her for his wife?

Felicity's fingers trembled as she dialed the number. Her stomach jumped with excitement and dread. As she listened to the phone ringing over the long miles, Felicity's heart pounded in anticipation of hearing Beau's deep voice.

"Hello." It was a young female voice.

"Cherry?" she asked, wishing Beau had answered. "This is Felicity."

"Felicity, hi!" Cherry was full of exuberance. "I've been meaning to call you for weeks to thank you. Our new ski shop opens next week."

"Yes, I know," said Felicity. "Alma told me."

Months ago, when Bob Peters was still pressuring Felicity to build a mall at the lake, he'd introduced her to Warren Cross. Warren owned several skiwear boutiques around the country and was looking for a place to start a new one. Felicity had convinced him that Jackson Hole was the place for him, and she'd recommended Cherry as a partner. She'd been delighted when they'd hit it off.

"We got a great location," Cherry went on. "A boutique in Teton Village went bankrupt and we—"

"Wait a minute, Cherry," Felicity interrupted. "Will you have to drive to Jackson every day?"

"No, that's what's so exciting," Cherry said delightedly. "Ash'll still work at the ranch, but he says we can live in Jackson. Except in summer during haying. And maybe Ash'll stay during calving. Of course, when he absolutely can't get through, Bobby Jo will be here to help. She's almost as good as a man."

Felicity felt the blood drain from her face. "What do you mean, Cherry?" She hóped her voice didn't crack. "Is Bobby Jo living there?"

"Oh." A long silence ensued. "I guess you don't know." Cherry paused again. "Beau, um, he and Bobby Jo...well, they go out a lot.... He's with her now."

Felicity chewed her lip. "When did he... I mean how long have they..."

"Well... for about a month after he came home from Florida, Beau just tried to drink Pinedale dry," Cherry replied. "Then he and Bobby Jo started going everywhere together. Right after the night the sheriff brought him home too drunk to drive. He was hurting pretty bad, Felicity."

Felicity's head was spinning. She was afraid to ask the next question, but she had to know. Her fingers tightened around the phone as she tried to keep her voice casual. "Are they engaged, or what?"

Cherry hesitated. "Just about," she said. "They act like it'll happen any day. I'm really sorry it didn't work out between you and Beau, but I guess you guys weren't very good for each other, huh?"

Felicity could hardly keep from slamming the phone down in Cherry's ear. She swallowed hard and forced a normal tone. "I'm glad things...worked out for Beau. Give him my best wishes."

"Sure thing, Felicity," Cherry answered. "Say, why'd you call in the first place?"

Felicity cleared her throat a few times. She really should talk to Alma about this, but she couldn't. She knew if she spoke to someone with more sensitivity, her anguish would be apparent. Felicity didn't want Beau to know how much she still cared about him when he'd obviously forgotten her so quickly.

"I just wanted to tell Alma that the lake deal has fallen through."

"That's too bad," said Cherry. "But maybe it's for the best, since you and Beau didn't . . ."

Felicity ground her teeth and went on. "I just couldn't accept the destruction of the environment that would be involved." Somehow she managed a strained laugh. "And if I didn't like it, you can imagine what Beau would have thought."

"Yeah," Cherry agreed. "He would've blown his cool."

"Tell Alma I'll write her with the details."

"Okay, Felicity," Cherry said. "I'll tell them the deal's off, right? Great to hear from you. Bye, now."

Felicity said a strangled goodbye and hung up. Cherry's words echoed around her brain, mocking her. Beau and Bobby Jo . . . Beau and Bobby Jo . . .

What had she done? Dear heaven, how could she have been so stupid! Had she really thought Beau would wait for her forever? He'd warned her not to take too long. What kind of fool was she?

The thought of Bobby Jo in Beau's arms soon turned Felicity's tears to racking sobs. She wailed and raged until her chest throbbed and her throat ached, but the pain in her heart did not diminish.

When she remembered the morning Beau had tiptoed into her room, Felicity's face burned with humiliation. She had given herself at last to the only man she would ever love, and he had forgotten her. Oh, why hadn't she listened to that inner voice telling her to wait?

She paced the room frantically. He'd promised to love her always. Surely not everything he'd said to her had been a lie. He couldn't have forgotten her altogether, could he?

She felt hope begin to grow. Maybe Cherry was wrong about Bobby Jo. After all, Beau had always treated Bobby Jo like a sister. Even Bud had said Beau didn't love her. Beau wouldn't give up on Felicity so soon, would he?

Maybe, just maybe, when Beau heard Felicity's message, he'd call. She sank back into the corner of the couch and stared unblinkingly at the phone, willing it to ring. *Oh, call, Beau, please. Call now. Even just to ask about the lake.*

Midnight came and went. Two a.m.—midnight in Wyoming—and still Beau didn't phone. As the sky was lightening with the new day, a fresh wave of sobbing seized Felicity. Beau was never going to call. He had captured her heart, she was his for the rest of her life, and he didn't even care.

Furious, agonized, exhausted, Felicity grabbed the phone and hurled it against the wall. Snatching up her plane ticket, she ripped it to pieces and threw them after the phone.

"I hate you, Beau DuBois," she shrieked to the empty room.

In her bedroom, Felicity flung herself across the bed and dropped finally into a fitful slumber. It was late Saturday morning when she dragged her weary body out of bed. Sitting in her breakfast nook sipping coffee, Felicity watched stripes of sun move across the floor. The pain in her chest still throbbed. It always would. She had to accept it, had to get used to mornings alone, life without joy.

Well, she decided groggily, tomorrow she would start accepting. Today, she would go to the beach and try to forget. If Beau didn't care, neither would she. She had her own life, and it wasn't *that* bad, she told herself. At least it was civilized and warm. She slammed the front door of her condo, knowing she didn't believe a word of it.

At the St. Petersburg beach, Felicity lay on her soft terry towel surrounded by white sand, her body slathered with coconut oil, forcing her mind to empty itself of all thoughts of Beau. The hot sun and restful sound of the surf breaking on the shore lulled her into relaxation.

The next thing she knew, she was being shaken awake by the rough grip of a policeman. "Miss," he said, "you're going to be badly burned if you don't cover up."

The tight hot feeling of her skin convinced Felicity he was right. She slipped on her short green cover-up, but her skin stung too much to zip it up. Felicity stuffed all her things into her beach bag, hurried to her car and blasted her hot body with the air conditioning.

By the time she reached her condo, all Felicity wanted was a nice cool baking-soda bath to soothe her stinging body. She pushed open the door, flicked on the lights and gasped. Sitting on the couch, looking more formidable than he ever had in Wyoming, was Beau.

For a frozen moment her heart stopped, the world stopped, and Felicity could only stare, her mouth open, her green eyes wide in disbelief. Had she conjured him up? Beau said nothing. His densely muscled chest rose and fell erratically.

A warm weakness spread along Felicity's limbs—was it pleasure? Pain? She couldn't tell. Clutching the door for support, she tried unsuccessfully to think straight.

"How... how did you get into my condo?" she stuttered finally, feeling like a fool. She couldn't have cared less *how* he got in—she wanted to know *why*.

"Your neighbor let me in." Beau's steely smile reminded Felicity of the day she'd met him in Jake Conrad's office. Why was he so angry?

He held up the torn end of her telephone cord. "Was this so you wouldn't have to talk to me, Felicity?"

He rose and came toward her. Wearing his familiar Levi's, his white cowboy shirt showing the dark curly hair on his chest, Beau looked exactly as Felicity had imagined him night after sleepless night. She wanted to reach out for him, but she felt rooted to the spot.

"You knew I'd call when Cherry gave me your message, so you ripped your phone out of the wall, huh? Couldn't you just have told me that your feelings hadn't changed?" He shook the cord under her nose. "Would that have been so damn hard?"

Felicity's heart was pounding like a jackhammer. Would Beau be here if he loved Bobby Jo? She was afraid to ask.

"I didn't rip the cord out of the wall, Beau. I just threw the phone across the room."

The hint of a grin crooked his wonderful lips. "Great," he said. "That explains everything."

Oh, how she wanted to touch him. "Did you look at those scraps of paper I threw at the phone?"

Beau glanced back into the living room at the pieces of ticket all over the floor. "I fly three thousand miles to see you, and you want me to do your housework?"

He was really smiling now and Felicity couldn't help smiling in return. No matter how angry he was, just being near him filled her with joy. She stretched a hand toward him. Maybe they didn't need explanations, just love. "Beau..."

Suddenly, Felicity was clasped in the strong arms she had ached for every minute since she'd left Wyoming. His lips covered hers and her knees gave way. He picked her up and carried her to the couch, his hand under her sandy thighs, his mouth never leaving hers. She melted against him, her heart rejoicing that he was here, that he was hers.

He lifted his mouth slowly. His inky-blue eyes pinned her with their intense gaze. "So, why'd you throw the phone, Easterner?"

Beau's deep loving voice started a warm glow spreading through her. Her arms stayed firmly around his neck as she answered. "Because you didn't call me back."

"But I did," he protested. "First thing this morning. I couldn't get through."

"See?" she said accusingly. "First thing this morning. After my heart was already broken. Why didn't you call me last night while my phone was still connected?"

Beau looked away from Felicity's demanding stare. "I got home at two o'clock. I didn't see Cherry and find out about your call until breakfast."

"Exactly," said Felicity. "Home at two o'clock. When you finally saw Cherry this morning, did you ask her what she'd said to me?"

Beau winced. "I tried not to think about it."

"She told me you were out with Bobby Jo and you were going to marry her." Felicity's stomach began to knot simply thinking about it. The warmth she'd felt a few minutes ago was gone.

"That's just Cherry's pipe dream," Beau said. "She feels guilty dragging Ash off to Jackson."

Felicity sat up stiffly on the couch next to Beau. "I waited until dawn for you to call, Beau, knowing you were with Bobby Jo. That's when I threw the phone."

Beau took Felicity's face between his palms. "Bobby Jo and I are friends, Felicity. That's all we've ever been."

Felicity shook her head. "Friends don't spend all night together. Bobby Jo has always wanted to live on the ranch with you."

"She wanted to live on the ranch with *anyone*. But when she found out how I really felt about you, she backed off. She thinks I'm crazy to want a soft Easterner dude." Beau stroked her cheek. "But she was worried about me after I came back from Florida. Especially after... well one night..." Beau looked chagrined at the memory.

"I know," said Felicity. "Cherry told me. But if it was just friendly, then why were you out so late? You didn't... you know..." Her cheeks flamed. "Did you... I mean..."

Beau pulled her back onto his lap. "Why, Felicity Walden," he chuckled, "are you asking me to kiss and tell?"

Felicity wasn't going to be drawn in by his infectious humor this time. "You'd better answer me, Beau. Why were you out so late?"

His eyes crinkled with laughter. "Maybe I'll tell you on our fifth anniversary."

Angrily, Felicity dug her nails into his shoulders, but Beau captured her hands and held them tightly in his.

"We won't have an anniversary. In fact," she insisted, her voice rising, "you won't have another birthday, if you don't—"

Beau's warm lips descended, stopping her words and starting that sweet familiar fire in her center. Finally he murmured, "Bobby Jo stayed out with me until I was so tired she knew I'd go home to bed, not back to Pinedale. She knows how much I love you, Felicity."

"Why'd you let me go on working on the lake project," Felicity asked, "even after Cherry met Warren Cross?"

A lazy smile curved his lips. "I didn't want you to forget me. I had to do something to keep your thoughts on Wyoming."

"I did think about you, Beau." She laid her cheek against his chest and listened to his heart beating. "I thought about you every minute. But what would you have done if I'd gone through with the deal?"

He stroked her hair gently. "I would've backed out at the last minute."

"What?" Felicity straightened angrily. "You'd have let me do all that work for nothing?"

Beau took her face between his palms. "I would have done whatever it took to get you back, Felicity."

Felicity relaxed against his chest once more, wanting never to move, knowing that this place in Beau's arms was her real home, no matter where she lived. "It was so frustrating," she said. "Thinking about you all the time and never being able to talk to you."

"I know. When Cherry told me this morning what you said about the lake, I knew I had a chance. When I couldn't call you, I..." His arms tightened fiercely around her. "I had to come convince you in person."

"Mmm," she said. "Convince me some more."

A sudden seriousness filled his eyes. "No," he said. "Give me an answer."

Felicity was startled. "You don't know?"

"I want to hear it."

"If you'd done my housework, as I suggested," she said, running her fingertips over his tight lips, "you wouldn't need an answer. Want to pick up those scraps now?"

His lips softened at her touch. "Just tell me what they are."

"That's my plane ticket to Jackson," she replied. "Or it was until I shredded it and threw it at the phone you didn't use to call me. I bought it yesterday. Do you think the airline will accept it this way?"

The smile breaking through Beau's tension made her heart catch. "I'll buy you another." He pushed the terry cover-up off her shoulders and wrapped his arms around her. "Now I want to hear you say yes."

"Maybe I'll say it on our tenth anniversary," she said gleefully.

Suddenly Felicity was flat on her back, looking up into Beau's dark eyes, his hard body pinning hers against the couch.

"Say it, Felicity," he said, trailing kisses down her throat. "Tell me you want to spend the rest of your life in the middle of nowhere—" his lips moved to the sensitive skin above her breasts "—with a stubborn rancher who will never change." He teased her quivering lips with his tongue. "Say it, Felicity, say it."

"Oh, Beau," Felicity gasped. "I don't want you to change. I love you. Yes, yes, yes!"

Many minutes later, Beau lifted his lips from hers and looked into her dazed green eyes. "I hate to bring this up when we've only been engaged for ten minutes," he said, "but you're all greasy and gritty...and you smell like a coconut."

"Cowboys," she murmured, nuzzling his bristly chin, "don't know a thing about getting a tan."

"Hah!" he declared. "Covering yourself with butter and sand is not the way to get a tan. Haying is the way to get a tan. Besides—" his eyes traveled down her body covered only by the tiny bikini "—you don't look tanned to me—you look red. But if you'll wash off all that grit, I'll marry you anyway. Tonight."

Her eyes lit up. "Tonight?"

"As soon as you change your clothes," he said, pulling her to her feet. "I'll call your parents while you're in the shower." He turned her toward the bedroom and began shoving her, gently but firmly, in that direction. "If you're not out of there in half an hour, I'm coming in after you."

"Half an hour!" Felicity resisted the pressure of his hands. "Beau, we can be married tomorrow."

Beau pulled her hard against him. "Woman," he said, suddenly serious, "I almost lost you once. I won't risk it again. This time you *will* do what you're told. An hour from now, you'll be my wife, and that's final!"

Felicity thought of all the pain she'd caused them both by her indecision. No wonder he wanted to get married tonight. "Yes, sir," she said meekly.

Beau laughed as he released her. "Why am I so sure," he asked the ceiling, "that this is the last time I'll ever hear those words?"

"At least you know what you're getting into," Felicity said as she headed for the shower.

IN HER DREAMS, Felicity's wedding had always taken place in that sweet little chapel at Indian Rocks Beach, not in Judge Wisdom's chambers. She'd always worn a lacy white dress, not a sky-blue business suit. But when her mind had tried to picture her groom, she'd never been able to see past the tuxedo. Now she knew why.

Because that faultlessly attired imaginary man was cardboard. The flesh-and-blood man standing next to Felicity now, the man who looked so handsome in jeans and a cowboy shirt, the man who moments ago had taken her hand from her father's, was so much more than the man in her girlish dreams that it took her breath away. Long white dresses and chapels full of guests paled in significance when Felicity gazed into Beau's dark eyes and saw reflected there all the joy she felt filling her own soul.

The judge, an old friend of her father's, cleared his throat. "Felicity?"

She glanced at him, hating to tear her eyes from Beau. Judge Wisdom was looking at her expectantly, his white brows raised. What had she missed? Her mother laughed quietly.

Confused, Felicity looked back to Beau. "What . . ."

A slow cherishing smile curved his lips as his eyes caressed her face. Taking her hands, he spoke softly, just to her. "Felicity Walden, do you take this man—"

The rush of love she felt was so intense, it almost burst her heart. "Oh, Beau, I do, I do."

"So do I, Easterner." He swept her into his arms. "Till death us do part."

From *New York Times* Bestselling author
Penny Jordan, a compelling novel of ruthless passion
that will mesmerize readers everywhere!

Penny Jordan

Silver

Real power, true power came from
Rothwell. And Charles vowed to have it,
the earldom and all that went with it.

Silver vowed to destroy Charles, just as surely and
uncaringly as he had destroyed her father; just as he had
intended to destroy her. She needed him to want her . . .
to desire her . . . until he'd do anything to have her.

But first she needed a tutor: a man who wanted no one.
He would help her bait the trap.

Played out on a glittering international stage,
Silver's story leads her from the luxurious comfort of
British aristocracy into the depths of adventure,
passion and danger.

AVAILABLE IN OCTOBER!

 HARLEQUIN

PASSPORT TO ROMANCE VACATION SWEEPSTAKES

OFFICIAL RULES

SWEEPSTAKES RULES AND REGULATIONS. NO PURCHASE NECESSARY.
HOW TO ENTER:

1. To enter, complete this official entry form and return with your invoice in the envelope provided, or print your name, address, telephone number and age on a plain piece of paper and mail to: Passport to Romance, P.O. Box #1397, Buffalo, N.Y. 14269-1397. No mechanically reproduced entries accepted.
2. All entries must be received by the Contest Closing Date, midnight, December 31, 1990 to be eligible.
3. Prizes: There will be ten (10) Grand Prizes awarded, each consisting of a choice of a trip for two people to: i) London, England (approximate retail value $5,050 U.S.); ii) England, Wales and Scotland (approximate retail value $6,400 U.S.); iii) Caribbean Cruise (approximate retail value $7,300 U.S.); iv) Hawaii (approximate retail value $ 9,550 U.S.); v) Greek Island Cruise in the Mediterranean (approximate retail value $12,250 U.S.); vi) France (approximate retail value $7,300 U.S.).
4. Any winner may choose to receive any trip or a cash alternative prize of $5,000.00 U.S. in lieu of the trip.
5. Odds of winning depend on number of entries received.
6. A random draw will be made by Nielsen Promotion Services, an independent judging organization on January 29, 1991, in Buffalo, N.Y., at 11:30 a.m. from all eligible entries received on or before the Contest Closing Date. Any Canadian entrants who are selected must correctly answer a time-limited, mathematical skill-testing question in order to win. Quebec residents may submit any litigation respecting the conduct and awarding of a prize in this contest to the Régie des loteries et courses du Quebec.
7. Full contest rules may be obtained by sending a stamped, self-addressed envelope to: "Passport to Romance Rules Request", P.O. Box 9998, Saint John, New Brunswick, E2L 4N4.
8. Payment of taxes other than air and hotel taxes is the sole responsibility of the winner.
9. Void where prohibited by law.

PASSPORT TO ROMANCE VACATION SWEEPSTAKES

OFFICIAL RULES

SWEEPSTAKES RULES AND REGULATIONS. NO PURCHASE NECESSARY.
HOW TO ENTER:

1. To enter, complete this official entry form and return with your invoice in the envelope provided, or print your name, address, telephone number and age on a plain piece of paper and mail to: Passport to Romance, P.O. Box #1397, Buffalo, N.Y. 14269-1397. No mechanically reproduced entries accepted.
2. All entries must be received by the Contest Closing Date, midnight, December 31, 1990 to be eligible.
3. Prizes: There will be ten (10) Grand Prizes awarded, each consisting of a choice of a trip for two people to: i) London, England (approximate retail value $5,050 U.S.); ii) England, Wales and Scotland (approximate retail value $6,400 U.S.); iii) Caribbean Cruise (approximate retail value $7,300 U.S.); iv) Hawaii (approximate retail value $ 9,550 U.S.); v) Greek Island Cruise in the Mediterranean (approximate retail value $12,250 U.S.); vi) France (approximate retail value $7,300 U.S.).
4. Any winner may choose to receive any trip or a cash alternative prize of $5,000.00 U.S. in lieu of the trip.
5. Odds of winning depend on number of entries received.
6. A random draw will be made by Nielsen Promotion Services, an independent judging organization on January 29, 1991, in Buffalo, N.Y., at 11:30 a.m. from all eligible entries received on or before the Contest Closing Date. Any Canadian entrants who are selected must correctly answer a time-limited, mathematical skill-testing question in order to win. Quebec residents may submit any litigation respecting the conduct and awarding of a prize in this contest to the Régie des loteries et courses du Quebec.
7. Full contest rules may be obtained by sending a stamped, self-addressed envelope to: "Passport to Romance Rules Request", P.O. Box 9998, Saint John, New Brunswick, E2L 4N4.
8. Payment of taxes other than air and hotel taxes is the sole responsibility of the winner.
9. Void where prohibited by law.

VACATION SWEEPSTAKES

MONTH 1 ENTRY

Official Entry Form

Yes, enter me in the drawing for one of ten Vacations-for-Two! If I'm a winner, I'll get my choice of any of the six different destinations being offered — and I won't have to decide until after I'm notified!

Return entries with invoice in envelope provided along with Daily Travel Allowance Voucher. Each book in your shipment has two entry forms — and the more you enter, the better your chance of winning!

Name _____

Address _____ Apt. _____

City _____ State/Prov. _____ Zip/Postal Code _____

Daytime phone number _____
Area Code

☐ I am enclosing a Daily Travel Allowance Voucher in the amount of **$**_____ Write in amount revealed beneath scratch-off

© 1990 HARLEQUIN ENTERPRISES LTD.

PASSPORT TO ROMANCE
WIN 1 of 10 Vacations
SEE INSIDE

VACATION SWEEPSTAKES

MONTH 1 ENTRY

Official Entry Form

Yes, enter me in the drawing for one of ten Vacations-for-Two! If I'm a winner, I'll get my choice of any of the six different destinations being offered — and I won't have to decide until after I'm notified!

Return entries with invoice in envelope provided along with Daily Travel Allowance Voucher. Each book in your shipment has two entry forms — and the more you enter, the better your chance of winning!

Name _____

Address _____ Apt. _____

City _____ State/Prov. _____ Zip/Postal Code _____

Daytime phone number _____
Area Code

☐ I am enclosing a Daily Travel Allowance Voucher in the amount of **$**_____ Write in amount revealed beneath scratch-off

CPS-ONE